Somewhere Quiet, Full of Light

Henry Corrigan

ISBN-13: 978-1-7637256-0-7

Edited by David-Jack Fletcher

Interior Design by David-Jack Fletcher

Cover design by

To my wife for her love and support and to my daughter for being awesome, rain or shine. I love you both. Always and always.

Other titles by Henry Corrigan

A Man in Pieces

SHARDS

Giving The Body (Book 1)

The Burden with Eyes Like Soft Fur

Money in The Mail

BEFORE MICHAEL CAME TO me, I thought I would be alone forever.

Please don't misunderstand. I'm not looking for sympathy when I say this. I was not bitter or resentful about my situation. I may have been old and lonely, but I was used to it by then. I am *not* one to be pitied, is that clear? I won't have it.

It was March when Michael arrived, the kind of day that's cold and blustery in the morning and damn hot in the afternoon. For someone like me who'd been left open to the elements in a hundred places, those days were the worst to survive, but I did it anyway. It wasn't in me to simply fall over. Not then, not ever.

For the thousandth time, I'd wished my family were still around to protect me, but they had been gone for years. They had become little more than glowing memories by then, but when reality held nothing but stagnation, my memories were the closest things I had to dreams, so I guarded them jealously.

To be fair, I was old enough that few people even remembered I existed, but those who did were not kind about it. Their little cruelties were much like the weather. Some natural force I couldn't control and which grew worse each passing year.

But it was on that mean, indecisive day in March that I heard the growl of an engine, throaty and sure of itself, heralding something big coming my way. From just down the road, I spied a large, crimson pickup truck wending its way toward me.

The truck kicked up an enormous cloud of dust when it stopped, but I didn't mind. I was too curious about the half-shadowed man studying me from behind the wheel.

After a minute or two, the man I came to know as Michael swung himself down from the cab. He was tall and well-muscled, his hair a chaotic black. He had strong hands too, the sort which were made for sanding boards or pounding nails flat. His eyes were a warm oak brown, probing but not unkind.

As the two of us stared at each other, you have no idea how much I wanted to hide the sorry state I was in. But I couldn't, not after this many years. By then, I sagged in more than a dozen unsightly places and my imperfections were countless.

But despite how tattered I looked, I put everything I had into standing tall because the pride of the elderly is no mean thing and I could still remember what it was like to be grand.

In those first tense moments, all I remember hearing was the *skrit* of Michael's boots and the creaking of my old bones.

Keeping his silence, Michael walked around me, his eyes picking out every detail whether I wished them to be seen or not.

And yet, on his fourth revolution, my heart lightened as Michael drew near.

Even before he touched me, I knew there was something between us. A connection. One I hadn't felt since my family passed.

The first time Michael caressed me, I shuddered, and he shook himself like a dog bounding out of a lake. He walked around me one more time and maybe it was wrong of me to let him know me so well but loneliness can make us do things we know we shouldn't.

Everywhere Michael went, my imperfections stared right back at him. My skin had peeled to tatters in every corner and I smelled of dampness and dust. But at the tip of my extremities, at one broken eye, that sweet, sweet man, traced an edge with his thumb and said, "You poor thing," in the deepest, softest voice I had ever heard in my life.

So right then, I didn't care if it was right or wrong. All that mattered was that we never be interrupted, which of course, was exactly when we were.

The car that came puttering up the road was as shabby as the man who drove it. Its windshield was cracked, its paint faded and one whole door was a different color from the rest. Its brakes shrieked as it skidded to a halt, and the sweating, balding man who leaped out was smiling so wide, I could see the back of his throat.

"Mr. Tillman?" he called, sounding so jovial it made me sick. "I'm Frank Welker, pleased to meet you. Sorry, I'm a little late."

"Thirty." Michael stared the man down.

"What's that?"

"You're *thirty* minutes late."

"Oh," Welker—the Little Nothing—said, pouting like a child who thought he could get away with anything. "Well, yeah, I'm sorry about that. My secretary must've written down the wrong time."

Michael glared harder.

"Well, anyway," the Little Nothing went on, rubbing his hands in what I'm sure he thought was eagerness. "Now that we're both here, why don't we talk about the old place? Beautiful, isn't she? Needs a bit of work, I'll admit, but you look like a man with an eye for—"

"Your office said this was an estate sale?" Michael asked, folding his arms across his expansive chest.

"Yep, that's right," the Little Nothing replied. If he bristled at Michael's interruption, he didn't show it. "Used to belong to the Miller family. They were, um...good people. Yeah, damn fine people, but the last of 'em, well... My office has been looking after it ever since."

"Uh huh. And by 'looking after it', you mean letting it sit with broken windows for years on end?"

The Little Nothing's pitted eyes could've driven holes through a tree, but his *happy* little voice didn't waver an inch. "Those are, uh...*recent* breakages, Mr. Tillman, I assure you. Everything was fine the last time I was here." Michael kept his silence and the Little Nothing's lips spun like tires caught in the mud. "I mean, you know how it is. Small town, big empty house. Kids look for ways to pass the time."

A stiff breeze came along and lifted a clump of leaves high into the air. The splat of them hitting the ground was the only sound.

"We'll get those windows replaced real quick, you can bet on that, Mr. Tillman."

Again, Michael said nothing. From somewhere in town, a car horn blared. The Little Nothing shuffled his feet.

"My office did the best it could!" he cried.

"Now, *that* I believe," Michael said at last, and the Little Nothing's relief was so great he burst out laughing. Fishing a set of keys out of his pocket, he put a hand on Michael's shoulder.

"You ready to see the inside?"

Michael brushed the hand off and stepped away. "No thanks. I've seen enough. I'll be in touch."

The Little Nothing blinked.

"Oh, but a piece of advice?" Michael called as he climbed back into his truck. "From one professional to another. If you really want to look after a place, you might want to keep the door locked."

With that, he drove away, his truck navigating the road with the same calm certainty as the man behind it.

Left alone, the Little Nothing didn't move until Michael was well down the road. Then he burst into a fury, strings of spittle peppering his chin.

"Bastard!" he screeched. "*Bastard!* Coming out here and telling me how to do my job!"

He kicked at the gravel until his breath whistled between his teeth. I think the only thing that pulled him out of his tantrum was the creak of my front door standing open.

Whipping around, the Little Nothing stared at me with eyes like burned matches but he didn't take one single step closer. Instead, he glanced at his car and I'm sure the idea was tempting. To simply run away and leave me to the elements.

But some of what Michael said must have stung because his voice turned reedy and mocking.

"If you want to look after a place you gotta keep the door locked. That's just my adviiiiice."

With one arm raised, the Little Nothing stomped toward me, as though I were his spouse who'd been cavorting behind his back.

But just as he came within arms-length, he stopped, his hot, angry eyes turning fearful as he sucked in a shaky breath.

This close, I could hear the thump of his heartbeat. I could look at his fingers and think of dry twigs ready to snap.

I wanted him closer. I needed to feel the crack of those digits, to hear him shriek, but even as I prayed for it, cowardice pulled him away, his legs shaking like rotten timbers about to collapse.

"Hell," he croaked. "To hell with it. I'm *done*." He made for his car and didn't look back until he was behind the wheel. The look in his eyes was priceless. As though he expected me to rip free of my foundations and come after him. I wish I could have but instead, I creaked for him, just once, which sent my 'owner' squealing away. His car fishtailed in the gravel as he took off.

It wasn't long before I'd put him from my mind but one thing I couldn't get rid of was the doubt of Michael's return. I'd spent too many years alone. I couldn't trust that he'd come back.

Two long, black weeks later, I was convinced I'd never see him again. That I'd wither away out here, forever.

But March turned into April, the cold gave way to sunny days, and Michael not only returned, he brought me something I needed the way plants need the sun.

He brought me his family.

2
ERIC

HOPPING DOWN FROM HIS husband's truck, Eric tried to figure out what the hell he was missing.

The house they'd driven more than three hours to see was so out of place it was almost comical. A massive Victorian monstrosity smack dab in the middle of two-story colonial countryside.

On the other side of the truck, Mike stood with his arms spread wide, face beaming as though the house were an old friend he hadn't seen in years. Staring at him, Eric knew the comparison felt silly, but he couldn't help but think of the secret glances a few boys in high school would throw at the star quarterback or the prom king.

"Well?" Michael asked, turning his way. "Whaddaya think?"

Eric kept his face pleasant and switched to 'helpful critic' mode in his head. Looking over the house was easier if he pretended Mike was just a fellow artist who'd poured his heart and soul into something he couldn't make heads or tails of.

"It's...it's *big*, bear. Bigger than you made it sound."

"I know, right?" Mike crowed, his face lighting up at the pet name. "Makes every other house around here look goddamn anemic."

"How old is it?" Eric asked, his stomach twitching at the question he really wanted to ask.

"Going on seventy. Can you believe it? I mean, just *look* at it!"

"I'm looking," he replied, while the words *and it will cost a lot more than you think*, skipped around in his head. "But won't it need a lot of work?"

"Not as much as you'd think," Mike said. "Give me and the boys a couple of months and you won't even recognize it."

"Okay. But what happens after those couple of months?"

"What do you mean?"

Eric searched Mike's face for any sign that he'd caught his meaning and then he bit his lip. "I mean, how're we gonna keep up with this place? The houses we grew up in *combined* weren't even this old and our parents still ran around trying to fix stuff."

"Eric, she's solid right down to the ground. We won't need to keep up with her."

"Mike, stuff always breaks in houses. And in old houses even more."

"I don't need you to tell me that. This is what I *do*, remember?"

From there, they lapsed into a silence so familiar it was painful. It still amazed Eric that, for all the years they'd spent scraping up nickels and pennies, they'd never fought this much. It was only once they got a little scratch to their names that short tempers and snappish comments fast became the norm. Not wanting the moment to get any worse was what made Eric bite the inside of his cheek until he saw stars.

Keeping Mike in the corner of his eye, Eric studied the house and fought not to cringe at the garishness which leaped out. The walls were red brick, the roof gabled and there was even a minaret though it had turned a deep shade of brown from years of dust and dirt.

The windows that weren't broken were etched with elegant patterns, while one or two on the second floor had extravagant, rusted ironwork curling around them.

Weeds crowded the base of the house like the hem of a ruffled skirt and what looked to be a whole generation of spiders had built their nests in the eaves. With his eye hopping from one pointed gable to the next, Eric tried to keep one thought in mind. Mike wouldn't have brought them all this way if he didn't think it was worthwhile. But the longer he looked, the more his concerns deepened. As if sensing his struggle, Mike put an arm around him.

" Scrib, they're asking peanuts for this place and I *know* I can talk that idiot realtor down even more. You should've seen the guy. He looked like he was ready to pay *me* just to take it off his hands!"

"But doesn't that bother you? A place like this being empty for so long? We're only a couple hours outside the city. Why hasn't some hedge fund manager snapped it up?"

Mike shrugged, impatient. "Maybe he just didn't want to put in the work. Who cares? That just makes it a better deal for us."

"Bear, this is a *ton* of work. The upkeep alone will be a nightmare and— Wait a minute. You said this place was built seventy years ago. Didn't the Victorian Era end way before that?"

Mike nodded. "Yeah, it did, but so what? It just gives this place more character."

Eric tried for a small smile, a peace offering in the hope that it would pull them out of bad habits. "You always told me 'character' was what hipsters were looking for. I didn't think we were all that trendy."

For half a heartbeat, he thought the peace offering might've taken hold. The corners of Mike's mouth twitched, and there was a welcome sparkle back in his eyes. But before Eric could even treasure the sight, it bled out. Mike's face twisted into a sour frown.

"Scribble, we can handle it, okay? I don't need jokes right now. And I definitely don't need us missing out on what could be a huge—"

A door clicked open behind them and they turned, both of them conjuring up smiles as Emily shimmied out of the cab. Dressed in pink, spangled sneakers and a coat she'd begged them to buy, Emily gave a joyous stretch, shaking herself from head to toe.

"God, that sucked," she groaned, letting her arms flap at her sides. "I thought we were gonna die in there."

Mike chuckled as he watched Emily stretch again, which helped to ease the squiggly feeling in Eric's belly. "It's called the Goddamn Belt Parkway for a reason kiddo," he said, smiling. "God left it to humanity so we could get a look at Hell before we die."

Eric rolled his eyes. "Nice. Real nice."

"What?" Mike gave him that innocent, puppy look, the shadow of a small smile emerging once more.

"It's okay, Papa," Emily chimed in. "I know they don't have Cracker Barrels in Hell."

Emily smiled and held up the Invisible Ink pad she'd picked up when they stopped for lunch. Eric wished they could go on like this, joking and enjoying the day, but Mike had come too far to contain himself. "Okay, now that we've survived Hell"—he pointed one long arm at the house—"what do you think? She's great, right?"

Emily stared at the house like a sailor lost at sea, searching in vain for familiar constellations. "Where's the..."

"Where's what, sweetheart?" Eric asked, watching her closely.

"Where's the... I don't know... *Everything*?"

"What do you mean?" Mike asked, his voice full of concern.

"I mean, there's nothing here," Emily said, sounding pained. "You said we'd be just outside of town."

"We are," Mike replied, patting the air. "You're just too used to everybody being on top of each other. Town's right there."

Emily's eyes bulged in horror and Eric couldn't blame her. Town was several miles away. "That's town? That's like...our nearest neighbor? How am I supposed to get to school? Hitchhike?"

Mike looked like *he* wanted to roll his eyes. "A bus passes by every day at seven. And if you miss it, so what? Is walking really that terrible?"

"It is if I get carried off by hillbillies," Emily said, giving the trees a suspicious scan.

"There are no hillbillies in upstate New York," Mike replied. "They're all in West Virginia."

A deep sigh. "Then they'll be well-educated hillbillies. Probably quote the *New York Times* while they're butchering me."

Eric couldn't help laughing. The sensation, the sudden burst of relief it brought was too good not to follow. Looking into his daughter's gray, mock serious eyes, he gave Emily a conspiratorial wink. Not for the first time, he marveled at all the years that had passed.

God, how do I have a kid about to start high school?

Emily looked barely into her teens but she wore elegant, gold hoop earrings along with that stylish coat which had made Eric hiccup while purchasing it. And that was before they'd decided to throw in the purse to match. At the time, it was all justifiable. Emily had worked hard, staying on the Honor Roll for all of eighth grade while somehow managing to *not* be one of those kids who fought her parents on everything. From a parenting perspective, Eric called it a miracle and counted his blessings. But old habits, good and bad, really were resistant sons of bitches. Despite what money they'd made, Eric still couldn't go to the grocery store without that familiar fear twisting its way through his stomach when it came time to turn over his credit card.

What also didn't help was that for all his good intentions, they failed to detract from the cartoon animals frolicking on Emily's T-shirt or the glitter that still clung to her shoes. Emily stood with a slight stoop which Eric hated because he knew it far too well.

Though she wasn't quite Mike's height, she'd been a good few inches taller than all of her classmates, even in grade school. And there were days when Eric could still feel *his own* mother's hand on his shoulder, silently telling him to make himself small so she could strut her way forward to shine. This, combined with Emily's tentative step, gave her the appearance of a girl trapped between two different ages, in a desperate search for what would pull her from one to the next.

"Haha," Mike said, rolling his eyes at last. "Look, I know it's out of the way, but isn't this what we've always talked about? A place away from the neighbors with lots of land for you guys to run around on?"

Eric shook his head. "We talked about a *little house* with a *big yard*, bear. I don't know about you but I was thinking half an acre, tops."

"Okay, so it's big. We'll grow into it."

Eric bumped him with his hip. " Bear, *two* families could hunker down here and one wouldn't run into the other until New Years."

Mike threw up his hands, trying for good-natured exasperation. "So, I'll leave a trail of breadcrumbs! That won't be so bad. One to the fridge and one to the bathroom. What more do you need?"

Eric didn't miss a beat. "The idea that if I screamed for help it wouldn't take our neighbors a week to hear me."

At that Mike *finally* cracked a smile and Eric tucked his head against his husband's neck. He let the moment stretch for no other reason than because he hated raining on Mike's parade, but for as much research as Mike must've done, Eric couldn't see any way around it.

"It's not just the size that's the problem, bear. Or how old it is. Emily's right, we're on the other side of everything out here. The kids will have to deal with new schools, new friends. How are we gonna—"

"Yaaaaaahhhhhhhh!"

All three jumped as, with a thundering roar, the fourth member of their clan leaped out of the truck and tore across the grass, skewering invisible enemies with her plastic sword along the way.

Skidding to a stop like the world's tiniest conqueror on eight year old legs, Iris turned with a flourish and sheathed her sword.

"Papa, I'm hungry," their little Napolean declared, both hands on her hips. "Can we have a snack?"

The three subjects laughed so hard, they needed to lean on each other for a minute. Emily was the first to shake her head.

"You goofball!" she shouted, while Mike pressed a hand against his ribs.

"Well, I'm... I'm counting that as *one* vote in favor of this place," he said.

Eric wiped a tear out of his eye and bumped him again. "Yeah, too bad for you her name's not on any of the accounts. We'll eat soon, sweetie! Papa and Daddy need to finish talking first."

Iris accepted this with grace, then charged across the yard to savagely attack a tree.

"Stay where we can see you!" Eric cried, to which Iris let out a war whoop in reply.

"I'll keep an eye on her," Emily said, pulling herself free. "You guys let us know when you decide where we're gonna be living."

Eric and Mike waited 'til she was safely out of earshot, then Mike's face became earnest as he looked back at the house.

"We've got to do this, Scribble. We'll never get another chance like this."

"Mike..." Eric began, disliking the drawn look to his eyes.

"Just listen for a minute, okay?"

Eric's cheek hurt too much to bite it again, so instead he settled for cracking his knuckles. It was the closest he could come to keeping silent. If the sound bothered Mike, it didn't show on his face. Instead, he dug his callused thumbs into his temples, ordering his thoughts. "Eric, I'm tired of living in apartments. I'm tired of us being crammed into two little rooms. I'm *sick* of our landlord screaming at all hours of the night."

Eric put a hand on his shoulder. "I know, Bear. I am too. But this will eat up most of our savings and that doesn't even include upkeep."

"Scrib, I've been renovating other people's houses for years. This is our chance to *finally* build something for ourselves." Scribble and Bear, were pet names they'd chosen for each other years earlier. One of those things that neither remembered where it began, but it had settled into second nature now.

Mike swept one long arm out showcase style, but for as much as Eric wanted to share his enthusiasm, this wasn't going to be another project to fix up and sell. This would be their *home* and Eric's stomach turned at the thought of even walking through the door. After a lifetime of worrying about money, he couldn't even look at the house without thinking anything but... Eric blinked and rubbed his eyes, his vision blurring as floaters, microscopic dust bunnies drifted by.

Beside him, Mike was too caught up in his own argument to stop, his voice rising as he laid out 'their' plan.

"...telling you, she's like bedrock. Her foundation could withstand mortar fire. If we get everything updated and landscaped, in a year or two she'll be worth three times what she is now. We can't pass this up. If we're going to buy a house then let's go for it. Stop worrying about the money and just let me..."

3

ME

EVEN AS MICHAEL WENT on, I could see he wasn't wearing Eric down. Each time that sharp-eyed, sandy-haired man looked at me, his face closed up shop, like a merchant turning off the lights at the end of the night. Terrified my future might be slipping away, I stretched myself as far as I could.

Through our connection, I knew that for Michael, I was a chance to lock the door and tell the rest of the world to go to hell. His hopes and fears were like the beginning of a bonfire, warm and inviting sparks that were growing steadily. All I had to do was keep him close and one day the flames would tower twice as tall as a man, their light seen from miles away.

With Iris—dear, sweet, screaming Iris—her dreams were like a road flare. Small but so bright I couldn't look at them directly. To her I was a battlefield, a castle, a city she could defend. She'd wanted room to move as long as she could remember and was as happy here as anywhere.

Emily, for her part, was almost as simple as Michael or Iris. She was like a searchlight trying to gaze in every direction at once. She was so desperate to belong somewhere that it took little for me to catch her attention and tether it like a boat adrift on a lake. With a gentle tug, Emily's whole body twisted round to stare at me in wonder.

But Eric...

Eric was by far the hardest to reach. His dreams were like the glow of a porchlight, warm and welcoming, but fixed in one place. I couldn't move him an inch, but the longer I looked the more I knew I didn't have to. He might've looked at Michael with kindness but guilt was there as well. He *hated* squashing Michael's dreams, hated the miserable look on his face and that simple regret was all I really needed. I didn't have to convince him I could be good for them. His guilt would do that for me.

The moment Eric's face softened, Michael seized upon it. He spoke faster, with more urgency, and my heart leaped as his words seeped through. Even as he drew Eric closer, all but crushing him against his larger frame, Michael never stopped looking at me as if I was the greatest thing in the world. Which I was, or at least I would be. Because despite Eric's fears, I *was* the best thing for them.

They just didn't know it yet.

4

ERIC

MIKE KEPT TALKING, BUT for as hard as he tried to listen, Eric lost everything except the sound of his voice. A memory intruded, old but shining bright, and the more he rubbed his eyes, the more it sharpened. He remembered Cheese and Bread Night from long before Iris was even a thought.

Emily had been what, three? No, four years old. It was the end of summer, preschool only a few days away and it was still hot. The kind of day when every minute spent outside was like being wrapped up in wet laundry that also happened to be on fire. Emily woke up crying early that morning, terrified of new teachers, a new school and being away from Papa and Daddy. Mike had been up late going over plans for a new renovation and Eric had woken up twice from nightmares about bills and the new school year.

Between their daughter's school supplies and his own art supplies, it was a hellish time.

Looking back, he could see the escalation , he knew there'd been real growth, sacrifices which took root and were reaching higher every day. Mike's business was taking off, his own art gaining word-of-mouth, but with their credit cards at max and the price of paint going up along with everything else... By five o'clock that night, it had already been a long, weary day and that was *before* Eric discovered the gray, moldy hairs on the leftovers he'd meant to use for dinner.

"Goddammit!" he cried and then instantly regretted it as Emily retreated around the corner, tears shining in her eyes.

"I'm sorry, baby," Eric said, his heart breaking a little at the way Emily *didn't* come closer.

Mike had to scoop her up in his arms and nuzzle his nose into her hair to get her to calm down. "It's okay, kiddo." His voice was soft. "It's just been a long day for all of us. Squeezy hug?"

Emily nodded, her fear drifting away like a summer storm on its way to the horizon. Mike hugged her tight, then carried her over to peer at the leftovers.

"Hoo boy! Okay." He chuckled, throwing his free arm around Eric. "So... How about we hit up the diner?"

Eric had wanted to bite his arm off at the shoulder. "We don't have the *money*," he snapped, still too upset to do anything else.

Mike may have been taking his life in his hands then, but he kept his arm there all the same. " Scribble, the bills are covered, we've got a little cash from your last painting and I don't know about you, but I'm not really interested in cereal tonight. Throw that out and then grab your coat, I'll get Emily together."

Eric didn't remember agreeing. All he could conjure up was the stench of rotten meatballs and the way the mold floated like islands across the sauce.

The Empire Hill diner was the sort of place he'd been thankful for ever since he was a kid. The kind where the portions meant leftovers for days, the desserts were a meal in themselves, and they filled up his coffee cup until he was a wired, jangly ball of "Ahhh! What is happening?"

That night, they took a table close to the dessert case, Emily in a chair of her own because she was already too tall for booster seats. They'd looked at the menu and Eric was both starving and not. His stomach growled at the burgers and club sandwiches, thick, generous things piled with bacon, pickles, and lettuce. It even rumbled at the soups, despite the heat, his tastebuds bursting to life at the thought of a heavily-spiced Manhattan clam chowder. But even as his stomach all but chewed on the table, his eyes widened at the prices. He'd been so concerned about money, in fact, that he'd completely forgotten to ask the most important question of all. But thankfully, Mike was there to save him.

"Hey kiddo, what would you like for dinner?"

Eric imagined any parent of a four-year-old knew just how loaded a question that really was. Emily was at the age when there were few things she was comfortable eating and there'd been more than enough fights at the dinner table. But right then, Emily, who'd been beaming as she colored with the two tiny crayons the diner provided, took one look at the menu and said, "I will have cheese."

Mike, thank goodness, was able to laugh. Because it took everything Eric had not to slap the table.

"How...how about a cheese sandwich, sweetheart?" Mike asked, tucking a stray bit of hair behind their daughter's ear.

Emily shook her head hard. "No."

Squeezing his eyes shut, Eric rubbed them with his thumbs. "Emily, you can't just have—"

"How about this?" Mike said, saving him again before his bad mood got the best of him.

Looking up at Mike, Emily's eyes were wide and cautious.

"How about cheese and bread?" he asked, casting a warm smile at her. Eric would never know how he managed to look so patient after the day they'd had.

Emily thought about it for a second. She looked up at the ceiling, her little pink tongue licking her lips, then nodded. "Okay," she said, before going right back to coloring as if it all had been no big deal from the very beginning.

Their waitress came by then, and the muscles in Eric's back tightened. He loved the Empire Hill, but they'd had some problems there too. Last time, their waitress had been a sour, pinched-face woman who took one look at their family and couldn't wait to shove them out the door. Eric had complained to the manager, who apologized, but it still ruined what should've been a happy night for all of them.

As near as he could tell, the other waitress was gone, or at least not working that night, which made Eric feel better. But even still, he couldn't keep a little bit of dread from curling its way up his spine as he studied the woman in front of him.

Stopping just short of bumping into their table, the waitress pulled out a pad and pen with practiced ease. "Evening everybody! How we all doing tonight?"

Despite his fear, Eric found himself relaxing. Their waitress was a stout middle-aged woman who looked like she always kept a smile right at the edge of her lips, just in case it was needed. She flashed each of them one of those professional smiles and looked, for all the world, like someone who didn't give a damn what kind of family they were, one way or the other.

After a heartbeat, Eric smiled. "We've been having a tough day. How about yourself?"

Their waitress laughed. "Oh, about the same. It seems to be catching," she said, her voice both tired and happy at the same time.

Eric chuckled, the muscles in his back slowly unknotting. "Yeah, unfortunately."

"My name's Charlene," the woman went on. "What can I get for ya?"

Emily glanced up as if on cue. "I'll have cheese on bread," she said, in that guileless but confounding way only kids could pull off.

Charlene, bless her, didn't even looked confused, just caught Mike's eye as he mouthed the words, "Grilled cheese."

With a wink, Charlene nodded, her genuine smile ticking up a few degrees. "Cheese and bread it is. What do you think, darlin'? Cheese and bread for the whole family?"

Emily's face lit up, looking so elated to have someone take her seriously that she began to beat her little fists against the table. "Cheese and bread! Cheese and bread! Cheese and bread!"

Mike laughed until tears welled and Eric joined with him, but it was Charlene throwing a guffaw into the mix that really sealed the deal for them. That night, Emily gobbled down a grilled cheese sandwich the size of her face. Mike tore into a cheeseburger with extra cheese, and Eric did savage things to a bacon cheeseburger with extra bacon *and* extra cheese.

Thanks to the laughter of that night, and the kindness of it, Eric not only got his appetite back, but found it had been supercharged along the way. To the point that they all split a piece of blueberry cheesecake, Emily pushing the blueberries out of her way only to chomp down on a mouthful that was dripping with sauce.

"Daddy can have the berries," she said, pointing at Mike, her face a riotous mess. "I just want the flavoring."

Mike ate her blueberries with a broad smile. "You got it, kiddo. Love you."

"Love you too. And Papa."

Eric's whole chest brimmed with warmth at that. "And I love you…" he said, before stealing a blueberry from Mike. "Both of you."

They laughed together one more time, the sound making everything seem possible in a way nothing else could.

It was a good memory, one Eric had stored away for moments just like this, all these years later. Just by closing his eyes, he could still taste the tartness of blueberries, the saltiness of bacon, and all that cheese. But as the memory faded, and Eric's awareness returned, it was Mike's voice which drew him back to the world again.

" Scribble, we can do this. A month to gather supplies, two months of work and we'll be ready to move in. That's enough time for us to pack, tell our landlord to go to hell, *and* register the girls for school. It's perfect. You couldn't ask for better."

It wasn't what Mike said that ultimately got to Eric, it was a combination of things. An amalgam built upon the memory of Cheese and Bread Night, the earnestness in Mike's face, and the guilt Eric harbored at the way they'd been arguing for far too long. Wasn't it just a few minutes ago that they'd laughed until they had to lean on each other to keep from falling over? Couldn't they get back there somehow?

Was the husband who'd saved him that night, and on countless more, still in there, waiting to be found again? Or was he... Eric couldn't bring himself to finish the question. Not then, maybe not ever. But whether he was ready for it or not, deep down he knew the question *needed* answering, if for no other reason than because his guilt wouldn't let up.

So...mixing up a pleasant, hopeful face from the color palette in his mind, Eric leaned into Mike, then kissed his cheek. Mike, who'd been talking nonstop, looked down at him in surprise. Those dark eyes of his dug in deep and for a moment, Eric had the sense Mike was testing him right down to the foundation. But as he slowly began to nod, Mike's eyes brightened and he finally smiled.

"Is that a yes?" he asked, his face full of a conquering hope.

Eric swallowed, choking down his fears as best he could, and said, "...Yes."

The *whoop* Mike let out almost cut through every single knot in Eric's stomach. Almost.

"YES!" Mike roared, both arms up in victory. He grabbed Eric's hands and danced him around, their feet crunching through the gravel with every turn.

"Girls!" he called, not taking his eyes off Eric. "Hey, guess what?"

The kids, Eric noticed then, had been staring fixedly at the house, but shook themselves before bounding over.

"Are we staying?" Emily asked, and Eric couldn't help but be confused by the way his daughter smiled. Hadn't she just been ready to hitchhike all the way home?

"We. Are. Staying!" Mike crowed, hacking off Eric's doubts at the knees. "Welcome to your new home girls!"

"Yaaaaah!" Iris cheered, doing the sort of uncoordinated happy dance that all eight year olds knew. "Can we have a snack now?"

That got them laughing, and Eric loved the way their voices melded together, like they were back on the right track again. "Yes. Yes, sweetheart, we can have a snack now. Let's see what we've got."

Eric rummaged through the cooler, too full of competing emotions to frown. They'd done real damage to their supplies. The juice boxes were gone, the pretzels depleted, and the peanut butter crackers were no longer as appealing as they'd once been. It was a long drive back to the apartment and it was getting near lunchtime already. But Eric decided he wasn't going to worry. At least not yet. Instead, he poked around inside his head until he dug up an easy wink and then directed it at his family.

"Think I saw a diner on our way through town."

Mike gave him a knowing smile. "Sounds good to me."

"Yaaaah!" Iris cheered again.

They all hopped back in the truck, their laughter ringing through the cab like an iron bell. And as they sped off down the road, Eric told himself that even if this was a mistake, it was a mistake he could accept, because after all the sacrifices they'd made...he could live with just about anything, for his family.

5
ME

THE PAIN BEGAN ONE month later. It was an agony that grew with every stripped bit of skin, every rotten bone torn out and every eye excised.

But for as unimaginable as it was, Michael stayed with me, his hands guiding me back to grandeur once again. Those hands erased my imperfections, they swept away dust and neglect. And as the days grew warm I helped Michael when and where I could. Muffling the sounds of the outside world, opening myself to let in the breeze.

But for me, the best hour of every day was always the last, because that was when Michael would send his crew home and the two of us could sit together in quiet solitude as the sun evaporated through a haze of purples and oranges. It was a wonderful time, one I cherished above all else, but it was not without its problems. Michael did frighten me once.

The sky had been a jeweled kind of black the night Michael rooted through the treasures my first family left behind.

He was in what he thought of as my basement where everything lay under tattered sheets and layers of dust. The Little Nothing may have been worthless, but he'd been right about one thing. My family had been good people, and they'd always be near and dear to my heart. Each piece Michael studied had a story behind it. And every story ended with their devotion to me.

Across from Michael sat the grandfather clock Mother had strapped to Uncle Lucas' back. I remember how he'd strained, almost bent in half, sweat pouring off his face. A few sharp words from Mother were all it took to get him moving.

Opening one of the glass front cabinets, Michael took out the crystal decanter little Millicent brought to me. The one she'd wrapped in her own coat to protect against the blood on her hands.

Ah, Millicent. Shy of Mother, I missed her most of all.

Uncle Lucas might've been amenable but Mother always had to cajole him into his duties. And poor Margaret... Well...she'd always been so willful. In need of so many harsh lessons. But still, she learned in the end. About the things we do for love. And perfection.

Michael spent several minutes wending his way through my little treasures, and I will never know why my body decided to creak when it did but Michael picked his head up at the sound and saw something I wasn't ready for him to see.

Some parts of me are secret. Precious. Only to be shared with those who are purely my own. And while Michael and I may have shared a connection...I couldn't risk it. Not then, anyway.

I shuddered as Michael brushed his fingers against a door I'd thought well hidden. I doubt even my 'owner' knew it existed, but to be fair, there were many things I kept from him.

As Michael moved the last few pieces of furniture out of his way, I summoned my influence.

The latch had rusted, and the nails were deeply set. The door didn't so much as quiver when Michael pried at it, which was a relief.

So close to my heart I didn't need to strain to see Michael's desires. They were almost as big as a bonfire now. Tall and blazing with leaping flames and I swept my influence across them like a wind scattering sparks.

Not there, Michael. Not yet.

Michael staggered a step. The light in his eyes flickered out and he stumbled like a man lost in the dark.

Almost blind, he careened into a corner and pressed his face against my cool stone walls. Into those shaky, empty places in his head, I drove in thoughts about the couches in the far corner and how they'd look in the drawing room. Or the idea that he, like Uncle Lucas, could heft the grandfather clock back up to its rightful place all on his own.

For the briefest moment, I thought he'd pass out. Just stretch himself along my floor until his crew discovered him in the morning. I'd pushed him hard and I knew it, but he was strong and after some time, he straightened up. And the second I saw his face I knew I'd done the right thing. Mother would have been proud.

The next day, when Michael returned, all thoughts of the door were gone from his mind. Instead he called out orders and I knew for the first time in years, I didn't have to fear the changing seasons.

From that point on, every day was a happy blur. I can't recall even one single moment of pain. What I *do* remember is the day it ended. The day Michael hefted in box after box and my life became laughter and chaos.

For every box Eric split open, there were a dozen more waiting. Pots and pans, toys and clothes, paintbrushes, bed sheets, photo albums, books. All of it was out of place. Each piece salvaged from imperfect lives and different styles, some of it close to falling apart.

But on that first day, with my family *home*, I didn't care. I let them run around as much as they wished, let them smile and shout and scuff me as they ran. I even swore to myself that I would let them be during the night. Allow them to dream among my quiet shadows, without a breath of guidance. Because there was time now. Time enough to mold them. To show them the means of proper living. I could afford to let them be their imperfect selves. For perfection, like love, would come soon enough.

6
ERIC

THE FRONT DOOR OPENED onto a grand foyer with the dining room to the left and a sitting room to the right. Up ahead, stairs led to the second floor where the bedrooms and library waited, all of it fronted by a long balcony railing. At the back of the house was a swinging door which hid the kitchen and a small half bath. They weren't in the door five minutes before Iris tried to claim the master bedroom as her own.

Their little conqueror hadn't liked hearing that the bedrooms were already assigned but when she found out her new room was twice the size of the one she'd shared with Emily, she allowed herself to be mollified.

But if Iris's room was big, the master bedroom could've slapped around their landlord's entire house. Halfway through unpacking,

Eric found himself looking for *more* boxes to unload, hating how old and worn their things looked next to marble countertops and four poster beds.

He tried to tell himself it was only the pressures of moving. That within a year, they'd have filled the space and in two they'd be looking for more places to store their stuff. But even after a mountain of paperwork, his hand cramping with each new document signed, he still couldn't believe they owned this house.

He wasn't blind to what it offered. Wrapped up in its hardwood floors and crown molding were good schools, even better neighborhoods, real vacations, and even retirement. Things *both* their families once thought were well out of reach.

Way back in high school, Eric's best friend had invited him and a handful of others over for dinner. It was supposed to be just pizza but his friend's mom had surprised them with a spread from this fancy Italian restaurant down the street. Chicken parm, sausage and peppers, crusty garlic bread, lasagna. They'd all been laughing and chomping through the first few bites, until his friend's mom started talking about some pain in the ass customer she'd dealt with at the bank. This woman, who had worn so many gold rings that she'd struggled to sign her name, complained for twenty minutes that the bank shortchanged her ten lousy cents.

This story soon turned into a lament and the words "money is the root of all evil" were uttered a few times. His friend's mother was a sweet, kind, well-meaning woman who would've helped out anyone she considered family in a heartbeat. But for Eric, who'd been staring at an entrée that could've fed him for the next three days, he had to bite his cheek to keep from telling the woman that only people who'd never been poor could say that. It soured what should've been a great time, because it only served to remind Eric of what was waiting for him at home.

There was a reason there were so many years between Emily and Iris. Between adoption fees, medical bills, and just getting their lives ready to involve a child, Emily alone came close to breaking them more than once.

Those years were long behind them now, thank god. Mike had a jeweler's eye when it came to abandoned places, and Eric's own art had brought them more than decent money, but it was an ingrained reaction built up over the course of their lives.

It was part of what *usually* made he and Mike work so well together. This shared want and desperation. But while Mike might've known what it meant to do without, Eric knew what it was like to live with someone who made things *worse*.

Mike's parents had been the kind of poor Hollywood never wrote about. Stooped, worn down people who never made it even with four jobs between them. Who avoided doctors and mechanics because they couldn't afford regular maintenance or prescriptions. Mike's father, a sweet, steady man with hands like rocks, passed in his early fifties. Eric had been amazed at how the mourners were divided at his funeral. Those with better jobs in better towns all shook their heads and said, "So young, so young." No one who lived like they did said anything like that. They already knew what killed him. They were just happy he'd lived that long.

At six years old, Eric wore hand-me-downs for a year because of his father's white Mercedes convertible. A thing he'd bought used then refused to part with even though every replacement part came at a ridiculous expense. Once, when he was nine, his mother spent half their grocery money on a coat she wore to a party with friends. The night she came home, she'd been so full of compliments, she almost floated through the door. Eric ate cereal every night for a week because of that coat.

Thinking back on his history, Eric's stomach clenched and he shook his head. Even with packing, unpacking, and the veritable mountain of ownership papers behind them, he still didn't know what it was that made him cave about the house. But caving was just how it felt. Like he'd allowed himself to be crushed beneath an enormous pressure and had been regretting it ever since. In fact, he couldn't understand why any of them cared so much about the place.

Emily had stared agog at it when they first arrived, while Iris was off conquering planets. Of them all, Mike had been the only one pained at the thought of walking away and while Eric tried to recapture the feeling that ultimately came over him, it only ended up running like watercolors dragged across the canvas. It all just dripped away, leaving nothing behind but muddy streaks.

Yes, things had been cramped in the apartment and he'd wanted to strangle their landlord every month, but there wasn't one single thing about the house that didn't make him think about that car and that coat. Things which had a tendency to own *them* in the end.

Taking a deep breath, Eric squeezed his eyes shut 'til red and yellow flares bloomed in the dark. Opening them, he pushed the black thoughts away by sketching the lights, turning them into fiery stars, overexposed faces, the silhouette of a man walking toward him, backlit by the sun. As the colors faded, Eric found that while the room was still large and cold, making their few meager things feel small, the break from his thoughts helped him not to feel small in turn.

Instead, he slipped a pair of scissors out of his back pocket, slitting open what he decided would be the last box for the night. Cracking open the cardboard, he smiled. Inside, wrapped in good, heavy cloth, were some of his oldest paintings, a few reaching all the way back to his teens.

For a moment, he thought about just putting the box aside, sticking it in a corner to be dealt with in the morning, but looking down at his old work made thoughts of new art leap up, like kids refusing to go to bed without one last story.

Hefting the box, Eric strolled out into the hall, hearing the whoosh of water off to the right. Glancing round, he found three closed doors. Mike in the shower at the very end, and the girls—if not asleep, then quiet—in their rooms across from each other.

Glad they had all reached the end of the day, Eric stood still and smiled. Then, turning left, he headed for the one room in this monstrous place that didn't fill him with dread.

In size and shape, the library mirrored the sitting room downstairs, squarish but with the Eastern wall bowing out into a large bay window. Bare of anything but his drop cloth, supplies, and easel, the room's built-in bookshelves looked lonely, though he doubted any of the books they brought with them could fix that.

In his younger days, Eric had dreamed of his own library. Each shelf crammed full of well-thumbed paperbacks, but much like the rest of the house, this library was *elite*. Its shelves so clean they would've hurled away anything that wasn't a hard-bound leather volume.

Setting his box down, Eric cracked open another, hauling out a stack of coloring books which he flipped through one by one, letting his eyes decide what he needed. The books were pure bargain bin stuff, no superheroes or Disney princesses, just roly-poly children, and animals in suits. Cheap things on cheap paper, bought three for a buck. He loved them because he'd hated them once. Hated that his mother refused to spend money on the name brand characters. Hated the look on her face as she handed them over, as though she'd been doing Eric a favor. The good mother buying her baby boy a treat. That was where Eric's artwork came from—anger and necessity. After all these years, the pictures were like blank slates, little stencils he could paint and bend and cut to his imagination.

Working fast, he cut out a pair and set them aside for the morning. A happy little family of four in a car with mirthful little house waiting for them on the hill. It may have been a little on the nose, but he had no illusions about his work.

Once finished, he switched off the lights and burped. The salty sweet acid of the bacon and garlic pizza they'd had for dinner told him that if he didn't take a shower tonight, he—and everyone around him—would regret it by morning.

Leaving the library behind, he grabbed a towel from the linen closet but stopped halfway down the hall. At the end, the bathroom door stood open, its light reaching almost to his toes and the rush of the water was louder than ever. With an unsteady heart, Eric stared, not sure what to do.

If it had been earlier in the night, or if the girls had been away at slumber parties, he'd have taken it as an invitation. A chance for the two of them to have some fun under the steaming hot water before tumbling into bed. But this late at night and after the day they'd had...throwing his towel over his shoulder, Eric poked his head into the light.

"Mike?" he whispered, surprised to find the shower curtain standing open. Without a body to block it, water sluiced into the cast iron tub, with a sound like someone beating a velvet-wrapped drum.

On a rack by the door, Mike's towel hung untouched but his clothes were gone and little wet footprints led back down the hall. Reaching into the shower, Eric switched it off, the spigot so hot he had to grab it in half turns or risk being burned.

Stepping back into the hall, years of thin walls made him resist the urge to call out again. Though with the house's timbers and stone, he was sure he could've screamed and it would've taken ten minutes for the sound to travel downstairs.

Back on the first floor, he found Mike by his shadow, those broad shoulders splashed in cartoonish strokes across the wall between the foyer and the kitchen door. His face was all business, his eyes trained on a blank spot on the wall, his bare feet turning to prunes as a puddle ate up the floor around them.

"Thing can't be that heavy," he muttered to himself as water sluiced off his chin. "I could move it if I had to. Just need a little extra rope," he said with resolve. "Now, where the hell did I leave that—"

With a well-aimed flick of his wrist, Eric dropped his towel on top of Mike's head.

Sputtering like a dog thrown ass first into a lake, Mike gaped at him, which only made Eric laugh all the harder, his hand flying to his mouth to cover the sound.

"I... I know you want to get this place fixed up, bear. But can you put off the projects long enough to finish your shower?"

Mike's mouth fell open as he looked at the towel in his hands. "I..." he began, then looked about himself, as though he couldn't believe what he'd done. "I was thinking about this clock in the basement."

Falling silent, Mike glanced behind him into the kitchen. Over his shoulder, Eric could just make out the basement door.

"I found it when we were renovating. You should see it. There's so much good stuff down there," he said, becoming more animated as he talked. "It's all handmade. Everything. And that clock. It'd look perfect right about—"

"Bear." Eric cut him off. "It's late and we're more than done for the day."

Mike turned back, looking disappointed, as though Eric had hurt him by not wanting to traipse through the basement at ten o'clock at night.

Before he could speak, Eric held up a hand. "Mike, I love you, but I'm not going into the basement unless the house is on fire. And maybe not even then."

Unsure what part of his words made it through, Eric was just glad when Mike's face softened, his eyes taking on the look like a man struggling to hold open a door while the roof was caving in.

"Sorry," he said, rubbing his eyes. "I just..."

Taking his hand, Eric led him up the stairs. "It's all right."

"No, it's not. I shouldn't have gotten so caught up. I just…" At the bathroom door, he peeled off his shirt, exerting real effort, the hairs of his chest matted into half broken whorls. "I want this to go right," he said, his face half-shadowed in the bathroom light. "Not just for me, but for the girls. For all of us."

"I know," Eric said, putting a hand on Mike's bare shoulder and kissing him. "I want that too. But enough for one day."

A moment after the door clicked shut, Eric heard the shower start up again. Now more tired than ever, he headed back to their room, resigning himself to a quick shower in the morning.

Once inside, the ginormous four poster looked more like a raft than a bed. Stacked atop a chair in the corner were the sheets that hadn't come close to fitting. In the end, the bed became little more than a collection of mismatched blankets with a few pillows tossed into the mix.

Curling up on his side, Eric tried to hold out as long as he could. Wanting to at least feel Mike's arms wrapped around him, the solidness of his chest pressed against his back. But as the minutes passed, the toll of the day came due, its charges weighing down his limbs, slowing his thoughts. He thought he heard the bathroom door open, heard the water rushing again, but he couldn't be certain. These sounds were hazy things, muffled.

He was dreaming before he knew he was asleep.

He woke before dawn the next day, beating his alarm clock by several minutes, his head full of a dream that ran like sand through her fingers. Clicking off the alarm, he sat up, his body telling him he could do with a few more hours sleep, but his brain wouldn't allow it.

In the near dark, he watched Mike sleep, his husband's body contorted like a car crash victim but his face as serene as Eric had ever seen it. Mike's left arm was hooked behind his head, right elbow pointing straight at the ceiling, his feet crossed at the ankles as though the lower half of him were sitting in a chair, waiting with infinite patience for the coffee to brew.

As he climbed out of bed, Eric had to fight the urge to pull Mike's limbs into some semblance of order. Slipping on his robe, Eric stepped out into the hall surprised at how warm the house was despite its size. In every corner and at every edge were the remnants of footprints. Dusty half shapes which marked the passing of their family.

Pulling himself up onto his tiptoes, Eric tried to remain silent, but then chided himself. Even just shifting his weight, the old floors groaned like hospice patients nearing their end. Suppressing a shudder, he peaked into each girl's room.

Waning moonlight filtered through their windows uninterrupted, the upper sky a deep purple black, the lower half turning red-gold, like the moments before an alloy forms. In both rooms, the beds sat beneath the windows and Eric felt a pang of guilt that neither of them had curtains. The early morning light might have been beautiful, but it poured in like a son of a bitch.

It was a strange oversight for a house so steeped in fake Victorian grandeur. In Eric and Mike's room alone they had curtains to spare. A thin blind butted up against the window, followed by a frilly white mess that looked to be made of muslin, and a tapestry-like outer curtain, all of it held up by a rod so big it could've doubled for power lifting.

But this wasn't the only thing out of place. The doors themselves, or the doorknobs really, were also odd, both of them set to lock from the outside. Eric had been with Mike long enough to learn a few things about renovating, so he could tell that the doorknobs were original to the house. But for as near as he knew, the girl's rooms were the only outliers. All the other rooms, including the master, were designed for privacy. These were meant for something else, and Eric wasn't sure he liked where that thought went.

He made a mental note to ask Mike about the doors and to get some blinds for the girls because Emily had one arm thrown across her eyes and Iris had all but buried herself in pillows. Peering in, Eric had to squint just to catch the slow rise and fall of her chest.

Clicking the doors shut, he threaded his way down to what he was already thinking of as his studio.

Here the light poured in, each pane cutting the glow into streamers until the sheer cascade of it pulled him towards the drop cloth and easel.

On the easel he set a standard eighteen by twenty-four inch canvas, but at the last minute he changed his mind, instead taking one of the larger canvases he would've reserved for landscapes at any other time. Once readjusted, he picked up the cutouts he'd clipped the night before and painted the back of each with glue. Narrowing his eyes, he surveyed the canvas, then smoothed them on, holding each down for a few seconds to make sure they stuck.

Once done, he forgot about the cutouts and relaxed his eyes until the cartoon figures drifted out of focus. Staring at the expanse of white behind them, he thought about the world he meant to create.

His mother used to say he worked ass backward, and it was true though he'd known better than to take it as a compliment. Eric's art always started at the edges, and rode the line between collages and actual paintings. In the tray of his easel sat a number of oddments. Pebbles and twigs he'd collected while out on walks, pieces of broken glass he'd found near twisted stop signs. Beside them was a small bottle of epoxy and a pair of tweezers, which he'd use to afix everything in place.

The glass would soon become the headlights on their car, the pebbles turn into the gravel of the road, but if he'd thought he knew how the picture would start, the larger canvas forced his ideas to change without permission. He'd meant to begin with warmth. Green and red, his favorite colors, then orange and violet, yellow and blue, but it wasn't until he reached for purple and gray that he realized more of last night's dream had stayed with him than he'd thought.

He did try to pick up the lighter, happier colors, but the attempt only left him feeling like he was four-years-old again, lying on the floor with his mother's hand on his wrist, forcing him to color inside the lines. The selfish and stubborn look on his mother's face as she tried to show off her 'little artist' to her friends. "Come on, Eric. Show everybody how good you draw. No, not that way. *This way*. Do it properly, for goodness sakes." After the 'audience' was gone, his mother had swept into the room, picked up all his coloring books and thrown them out. *"Why can't you just do what I say?"*

Eric knew of artists who could lose themselves in their art, sort of wander out into the forest and come back bearing fruit no one had seen before. But that wasn't him. He needed structure. Needed it the way people needed a loved one's touch. It helped him get a grip on the world in a way nothing else could.

In the dream something had been chasing them. A storm? Yes, a storm. No thunder, no lightning, just black from horizon to horizon. They'd been on the road, like the day before, all of them singing though he couldn't remember the tune. Mike's eyes were glued to the gravel, his smile like something he'd cobbled together for the girls as much for himself.

In quick, x-shaped brushstrokes, Eric rendered the storm in purple, gray and black, layering each until they ate up the sky, the stars and everything behind them. Beneath it he began to sketch out the road, the fields, the grit beneath their tires. He added ochre in for sand, holding his breath as he dotted in the pebbles and the fence post they slowly passed by.

In a persistent sort of hope, his brush started to move toward the lighter colors, mixing yellow with a touch of brown, then stirring up pink and bright, flaring orange to craft a sunrise halo around the car. But when he moved to touch the canvas again, he stopped. He found himself staring at the empty space surrounding the house and cleaning off his brush with a huff.

Playing his thumb along the bristles, Eric glared at the canvas as though searching for a way out. Before the move and all that came with it, his paintings tended to go one of two ways. Either he knew in exact detail how the picture would turn out, or it followed his instincts, letting color or shape lead him away. Even if all he ended up with was a mess, the mess would still say what he'd wanted to say better than anything else in the world.

But this time, staring at that mirthful house and its happy little family, he felt stuck, the dream telling him one thing but his gut telling him something else. A part of him wanted to reach for sweetness and light, but every time he tried, something tugged hard around his middle, like a leash keeping him from playing out in the road. Plus the more he thought about the dream, the more it came apart. Once their smiles had seemed so clear and sharp but now all he found was absence. There was no warmth here, only someone else's idea of a happy expression.

Blowing out a breath, Eric covered the canvas with a cloth. Stepping back, he tried to shake off his frustrations, focusing instead on the busy day ahead. The boxes left to unpack, the showroom's worth of furniture in the basement. More than enough to take up the day or even the summer if he was being honest. But still, he couldn't help but be disappointed as he walked away.

Taking the towel Mike had left behind last night, Eric jumped into a quick shower, the steaming water helping to wash away some, but not all, of his discomfort.

By the time he dried himself off, he wasn't the only one up and about.

Iris's door stood open, the room empty, his little warrior nowhere in sight. Heading downstairs, Eric put on a fresh pot of coffee to brew, his thoughts already turning toward breakfast. They didn't have much in the way of food, but they had the essentials, milk, eggs, butter, cheese, pancake mix with syrup and bread for toast. Enough for a damn good breakfast.

Gathering everything atop the marble island he set off to conscript Iris, who was already adept at making toast and setting the table while Papa got 'egg-goop' on his fingers.

With the scent of coffee following behind, Eric strode into the living room. "Iris?" he called. "Sweetie?"

No answer came and a slow circuit of the floor turned up nothing, even their boxes were undisturbed, playing sentry right where they'd been the night before.

In the kitchen, Eric looked out over the backyard, his anger rising at the thought of Iris gone a-conquering without asking first. Outside, the sun had painted everything in bright greens, yellows, and blues, its heat already seeping through the glass, but no matter how hard he squinted, the world was static. The grass unbent, the trees immobile, as though he were looking at someone else's painting, an artist who favored color but had no clue how to give it life.

He searched each room again, his teeth gritted as he did everything he hated, looking in the same place twice on the off chance he'd gone blind. The kitchen door flapped behind him, each revolution like a cheap pair of wings.

"Iris?" he called, no longer concerned about disturbing any-one.

Again, no answer.

His gaze turned to the basement door, his lungs hitching at all the stacked furniture, heavy glass and the thousand ways Iris could get hurt. He had his hand on the knob, about to call again when a clatter from the foyer drew him off.

"Iris!" he yelled, anger and fear curdling in his chest. "Iris, you know better. You know to answer when Papa says—"

Emily stood blinking at him from the landing, her hair disheveled, eyes wide, looking like she wanted to retreat back up the stairs.

"Hey," Emily said, holding very still. "Everything okay?"

"Where-is-your-sister?" Eric fired off so quickly it was almost one word.

"I...thought she was upstairs. Isn't she—"

"Iris!" Eric shouted, sweeping past Emily. "Iris, get out here! Now!"

He'd been about to shout again, to break into a run when he heard clomping feet and Iris came careening around the corner, half dressed, looking so worried she dropped her sword and sent it skidding down the hall.

"Papa?" she asked. "What I do?"

Where have you been? Eric demanded, hands on his hips. "I've been calling you for forever."

Iris looked, if anything, puzzled. Like she not only didn't understand the question but didn't know what to do with her papa either. "Huh?"

This made Eric feel so foolish that it pissed him off to no end. "Where. Have. You. Been?" He bit out, barely managing to keep from tapping Iris on the head with her own sword.

Iris looked back toward her room and pointed. "I was playing," she said simply, as if this answered the question instead of missing it by a mile.

Eric closed his eyes and rubbed hard at the bridge of his nose. "When I looked in on you before, you were gone. I thought you went downstairs."

Iris, looking even more confused, blinked at her room then at her papa. Finally, she shook her head. "Nuh-uh."

Eric sighed, still upset, but that feeling of foolishness won out. "Well, didn't you hear me calling you? Where were... *What* have you been doing?" he asked with rising disgust, only just noticing the state his daughter was in.

Iris wore a pair of jean shorts beneath a pajama top and she had one sock and one slipper on, neither on the same foot. The sleeve of her pajama top was smeared with gray dust and there was a smudge of dirt on her cheek.

"I was just playing," she said again before smiling widely. "This place is *cool!* Can we play hide and seek later?"

Despite himself, Eric felt his own smile curling into place. "We'll see, honey. We've got a lot to do today."

Pulling Iris close, Eric hugged her with one arm while wiping away dust with the other. "There," he said, . "Now, finish getting dressed, then come down and help with breakfast. Which do you want, eggs or pancakes?"

"Yes, please!" Iris cried and Eric laughed at their old game, a holdover from when Iris was too young to say she wanted both.

Patting Iris on the head, Eric gave her a little nudge before following her back down the hall. In a heartbeat, Iris broke off, both arms out like a starling as she swept back into her room, aiming to get dressed. At the door to the master bedroom Eric paused, amazed Mike had slept through all the ruckus. Running hand down the old wood, he thought about seeing if Mike wanted breakfast, but then decided to let him rest.

Their old kitchen table had been falling apart even before the move so they had a picnic on the floor instead. Emily dug out an old comforter while Iris set out plates and Eric grated a block of pepper jack. The stove may have been ancient but it worked better than the cheap clunker he'd fought with in their apartment. On one of its six burners, a large skillet of scrambled eggs came together, while fresh pancakes bubbled on the attached flattop. Working fast, Eric sprinkled salt and pepper into the skillet, flipped over pancakes, and then tossed a dash of cinnamon into a small pot of maple syrup he was keeping warm.

All told, the smells of brown batter, fluffy eggs, salt, and cinnamon were enough to make everything inside him growl, as if his very bones were hungry as well. While they waited, orange juice was passed around, along with a fresh cup of coffee which Eric set well away from Iris, who kept trying to sneak a taste.

In another minute, steaming plates were set before the girls and Eric smiled as they devoured them each in their own way.

Iris attacked her food much as she did everything, hacking at egg and pancake alike until they were all but indistinguishable, a consistency she seemed to enjoy more than either on its own.

"Gross," Emily said, while slathering a healthy dose of peanut butter on one pancake and jelly on the other. Smooshing both sides together, she took a careful bite, making sure none of it dripped onto her eggs.

Tilting her plate, Iris dipped two fingers into a pool of syrup and then grinned at Emily like The Coachman from Pinocchio.

Emily eyed those fingers and stared back daggers. "Try it and I'll hide your sword while you're sleeping."

"Nuh-uh!" Iris replied, which was somehow still appropriate though it made no sense. Tempting fate, she dangled her sword an inch from Emily's cheek.

"Not touching you. Can't get mad."

With the calmness of a seasoned yogi, Emily took another bite of her weird little sandwich.

Iris edged closer. "Oooooh, I'm not touching youuuuuu!"

Without even looking, Emily snatched the sword away and held it just out of reach. "Mine now," she said, still chewing.

"*Hey!*" Iris yelled, shuffling forward, mashing crumbs into the blanket like a steam roller.

Emily fended her off with one hand. "Nope, mine now. You'll never see it again."

"Papa!" Iris squealed, twisting in a million uncomfortable ways to try and get around her sister.

"Papa can't help you now! *No one can!* I am the sword bearer! You are nothing but my lowly squire, not fit to polish my—"

The last word turned into a squeal as Iris smeared syrup across Emily's nose, cheek, and chin.

"Ewwww! Papa!"

Eric had to set his cup down or risk snorting coffee into his sinuses.

He watched his daughters 'fight' for another minute, then separated them. Mike came sauntering in just as Emily was wiping syrup out of her eye.

"Okay. What did I miss?"

"Nothing," all three said in unison.

Chuckling, Mike shook his head. "Yeah, it sounded like a whole lotta nothin'."

Fixing himself a plate, he sat down with a heavy whump. Eric doubted anything was still warm but if Mike minded, he had two helpings of everything all the same. The next few minutes drifted by with talk of what needed to be done and when. The girls were assigned unpacking their rooms while the adults picked through the basement.

As everyone set off, Eric carried the blanket outside, unfurling it with a snap to send crumbs flying across the grass. Alone in the light, he imagined birds running riot but even squeezing his eyes shut, he couldn't hear a single chirp. Around him the trees stood still and the road lay quiet, the town nothing more than a muted backdrop. There wasn't even a smell to the outside world, just a kind of moist heat, making Eric long for the scent of flowers, or even dust.

Shaking his head, he refolded the blanket, then headed back inside. Not wanting to drag down his family's smiles, he conjured up one of his own, though the feeling of isolation remained. The sense that they were only things alive out here, well away from everyone else.

7

ME

CAN I TRULY BE blamed for what I did? When faced with Iris's smile and her limitless energy, was it really wrong of me to go back on my word? I don't think so.

I'd meant to leave them alone that first day, to not even stir a finger through their dreams. But from the second Iris woke up, her eyes blinking with excitement, I couldn't resist her. In the quiet of that early morning, I opened a hidden part of me, because not even Michael knew all my secrets then.

I can't describe how good it felt to see the gleam in her eyes. To watch her peel back the panel I'd cracked open for her. To watch her crawl forward, her sword tucked under one thin little arm. She didn't even hesitate, just started hunting through me like a true explorer. Ferreting out the secret places between each room, bursting through spiderwebs, brushing her fingertips along my ribs until I shivered.

As I watched her move, I could see a bit of a caretaker in her. Someone who, years from then, could take over once Michael grew too old and feeble. I imagined her bringing me little treasures, the way Millicent used to. Or perhaps, hauling up furniture like Lucas. She was already so strong, my little adventurer. I couldn't put it past her.

I was indulging her and I knew it. Perhaps a bit too much, but I didn't care.

I let myself lose track of the others, even Michael, though I passed him a few fleeting ideas. Which sheets hid the choicest furniture and what rooms they'd look best in. With Iris's playful squeals shrieking through me, it wouldn't be until much later that I realized my mistake.

How could I have known? I couldn't have, it's that simple. I couldn't have known that curious, incomplete Emily would ask to take her bike into town. If I had known who she would meet, I'd have ripped myself clean of my moorings and gone after her. But I was too lost and distracted by the joy of Iris, so what happened next cannot be my fault. For such is the power of love. It tells us everything will be all right, even as an older, wiser voice whispers that it will not.

8
ERIC

It was late afternoon when Eric found a hateful old woman and a wide-eyed teenager waiting for him downstairs. The teenager was on the porch with Emily, the two talking in awkward whispers, the space between them defined by how little they knew what to do with their hands. The old woman however, hung like an empress above the mantle in the living room, her face still haughty and garish despite having spent decades covered by a sheet.

Standing in the living room, Eric made a point of ignoring the old woman, and instead gave himself a chance to study the boy from shoes to crown. He was taller than Emily by an inch or so, but his wrists were the thinnest Eric had ever seen on a man. He had a shy smile but quick, intelligent eyes. The sort of kid who probably spent his lunch period scrawling in a notebook he'd never let anyone read...except for maybe the new girl who didn't quite fit in either. Eric smiled. Clocking the blue ink stains on the boy's hand and hearing no alarm bells, he decided they weren't about to run off and ravish each other, at least, not for the moment.

Turning his attention back to the old woman, Eric realized he'd never actually seen a family *portrait* before. He'd never known anyone who was rich enough to afford it either. But if the one above the mantle was any indication, he never wanted to see one again.

Hemmed in by a gilded frame, four people sat upon an overstuffed couch festooned with tassels, each of them staring out unsmilingly upon a world without an ounce of approval. Etched onto a small nameplate at the bottom of the frame were the words, THE MILLER FAMILY, DEIRDRE, LUCAS, MARGARET & MILLICENT. 1957.

Reading the year again, Eric shook his head. Despite living in the heart of John Wayne and Elvis times, every single member of the Miller clan were dressed like they'd just hopped off the boat from Victorian England. Hell, Lucas, a jowly man in his fifties, wore a top hat and monocle for god's sake, though for all the care he put into his appearance, he may as well have not been in the painting at all.

Without needing to be told, Eric knew which of them was Deirdre.

The woman standing front and center bore a sharp, narrow face, as though rather than having been born, she'd chipped away pieces of herself over the years. She couldn't have been more than fifty but while Eric was sure the artist had left out any fine wrinkles, he couldn't excise the superior cast to her gaze or the overbearing way she held herself. It would be like trying to pull a bone out of corpse, the two tied together by meat and sinew.

Deirdre's hair was black to the point that it blended in with the shadows behind her, and Eric couldn't be sure if this was a mistake or a sign that the artist had inserted their own bit of truth into the picture. Deirdre wore large, gaudy jewelry like she wanted the world to *think* she'd been wearing them all her life and she stood with one hand swept outward as if to say, *Look at me. Look at all that I have wrought.*

Before her, the three sat with perfect stillness, the youngest to her right, a girl of no more than ten, who was so ramrod straight it hurt Eric's back just to look at her. On the left was a girl about Emily's age, dressed in a cream-and-gold gown that made her look smaller somehow. Along with the gown came long white evening gloves and Eric couldn't help but notice the way she cradled her right hand in her lap as though she'd been grabbed by someone who'd wanted to hurt her and the gloves were meant to conceal the bruising.

Of the three, she was the only one not looking at the artist, her head canted to the right, unable to bear the thought of Deirdre's hand lying just beyond the scruff of her—

Crack!

Eric jumped, and had to bite his lip to keep from shouting . The noise, whatever it was, had shaken half the house. Running around the corner, he found Mike in the kitchen, shirtless and gasping over an enormous sea chest he'd dredged up from somewhere in the basement. His hands were shaking and there were livid red marks stretching across his back from the straps he'd used to haul the thing upstairs.

"Mike, what the hell are you doing?"

"I found it...downstairs!" he crowed, his grin like broken old pottery as he fought for breath. "Isn't it great?" he went on, missing that Eric didn't give a damn about the chest. "There is so much great stuff down there! And I know *exactly* where this is gonna go," he said, giddy with excitement.

" Bear, what were you thinking? You could have killed yourself trying to drag this thing up!"

"Wasn't... Wasn't that bad," he said, hands still shaking, sweat dripping off him which Eric was sure had to make the strap marks sting.

"Okay, sweetie," Eric countered, trying not to sound as pissed off as he truly was. "I think now would be a good time to take a break from the whole decorating thing."

"Whaddaya mean?"

"Are you kidding me? Seriously?" Eric ticked points off on his fingers. "You wandered out of the shower because of a grandfather clock, almost killed yourself hefting Davy Jones's locker just now, and hung a picture of the Crypt Keeper above the fireplace in our living room."

"Huh?" Mike asked, trying to both stretch and not lean back so far that he fell over.

Eric groaned and took Mike's hand, pulling him back around the corner to point up at the portrait. "What is *that* doing in my living room?"

To his credit, Mike studied it a moment, his eyes flicking to each face as though trying to remember whose side of the family they belonged to, his or Eric's. Finally, he shrugged and rapped his knuckles against the mantlepiece.

"This is where it goes. See? It's a perfect fit."

Eric blinked and drew in a nice, deep breath, unsure whether it was Mike's clueless response or the entire conversation that had him on edge.

"You know what else would be perfect?" he asked in bite-sized chunks , long past caring how it sounded. "One of *our* photos. You know, of *our family*?"

Having gone back to stretching, Mike gave the portrait one last, cursory glance. "We don't have anything that'd fit."

"Then put a couple in there! I don't care!" Eric exploded, happy to see any reaction, even shock, out of his husband, as long as it was one he recognized. "You can't keep dragging stuff up from downstairs and putting it anywhere you like!"

"I'm not putting it anywhere I like. I'm putting it where it *where it's supposed to be!*"

Mike was angry now, but while Eric knew they were shouting, he didn't really care. It was good to at least be on a playing field he had a chance of understanding.

"Mike, I love you, but everything you bring up is old, ugly, useless, or all of the above. What the hell am I supposed to do with a sea chest? I thought we were supposed to be selling this stuff. And I don't care what you say, I am not entertaining Emily's friend with Gruesome Gertie up there staring back at me."

"Emily's friend? What are you—"

Mike peered around the corner and had, what looked to Eric, like a seizure. Emily and the boy stood frozen on the porch, not even bothering to act like they weren't listening. Emotions flickered across Mike's face like static as he took in the boy for the first time. Surprise mixed with confusion, before congealing into a jaw clenching anger Eric couldn't remember seeing before in his life.

Stomping his way out the door, Mike crowded into the boy's personal space and crossed his arms with exaggerated menace. "What. Do. You. Want?!" he blurted, coming close to screaming the last word.

"Wh... Um. I'm sorry?" For his part, the kid looked too dumbstruck to be scared, even with Mike looming over him.

"Dad! What the hell!"

Eric flew outside in time to see the glare Mike leveled at Emily. Their daughter's head snapped back as though he'd jabbed her in the nose. She turned lost eyes to Eric who did his best not to look as confused as he felt.

"Bear ," he said , edging toward Mike while being careful to fold up his own anger and store it away for another day. "Let's take it down a notch, okay?"

He put a hand on Mike's arm, the skin so tense it vibrated beneath Eric's touch. Mike never took his eye off the boy and Eric didn't know whether it was his sudden anger, or the sweat still clinging to his skin, but the stench that roiled off him was so thick it had a taste to it. . An acidic funk that spoke of volatility and a need to be handled with care.

With slow, deliberate steps, Eric put himself between the boy and Mike, making sure to hold Mike's attention and keep his voice at an even keel. "Hi," he said to the boy, holding out his hand with as much congeniality as he could spare. "I'm Emily's dad. What's your name?"

"H-hi," the kid said, giving Eric a good handshake despite the nervous glances he flicked at Mike. "I'm, um... I'm Jason?"

"Hi Jason, it's nice to meet you. Do you live around here?"

Attempting a smile, the boy pointed across the distance to a white, two-story Cape just on the edge of town.

"Guess that makes you our nearest neighbor. How 'bout that?" Eric said, giving Emily a reassuring look. "Guess they're closer than you thought."

Emily started to roll her eyes, then cast a worried glance at Mike. "Yeah. Right. Closer. Now, I don't feel so *alone*."

Eric kept his eyes on the kids while the sound of Mike's angry panting subsided by degrees behind him.

"So, where did you two meet?" he asked, counting the seconds without an outburst in his head.

"The library," Emily answered, pointing to a tall stack of books sitting on the top step. "He was just helping me home with my stuff."

Eric glanced to the side of their porch where a pair of bikes leaned, the wheels not quite touching, much like the hands of their owners.

"Aw, that's so nice of you," Eric said, smiling and Jason had grace enough to blush.

"No big deal," he replied, and under better, less tense circumstances, Eric might've gone on grilling him until Emily died of embarrassment. But with Mike in if-he-moves-I'll-kill-him mode, he just pointed toward the pickup.

"Can we give you a ride home? It's too hot to pedal your way back and I'm sure your bike would fit."

He both heard and felt Mike bristle. The boards beneath their feet creaked as his weight shifted forward, his anger all but pulling at the hairs along Eric's arm like static.

Jason shook his head. "No thanks, that's okay. It's not that far. I can make it."

"Are you sure? It's no trouble," Eric said, more out of politeness than anything else.

"Yeah, I'm sure. Thanks again," he turned back to Emily who somehow managed one small smile. Jason ran a hand through his hair, a bramble like the color of sand after the ocean poured through it.

"Thanks for... Y'know, carrying my stuff. You didn't have to," Emily offered.

"No worries," Jason replied, smiling but staying where he was for a moment.

"I'll be at the library again on Friday. If you were thinking of stopping by or—"

Without looking back, Eric reached behind and put a firm hand on Mike, thankful that his touch was enough to let Emily's "Sure," pass by unmolested. Seconds later, the two made their goodbyes and then the three of them watched Jason pedal off.

When he was well down the road, Emily looked at Mike, her embarrassment giving way to outrage in a heartbeat.

"Dad. What was—"

"Go help your sister," Eric said, putting himself, once again, in the line of fire.

"What?!" Emily barked.

"Your sister can't find that shield your aunt gave her last Christmas. Go help her, before she tears the place apart looking for it. *Now.*"

Emily's gaze flicked back and forth between them, as though looking for someone to tell her she wasn't losing her mind. Not finding it, she growled like an orphaned cub and stomped away, her head battering ram low, her fists clenched at her sides.

Eric waited until she was upstairs before turning to Mike.

"Okay. Now, do you want to tell me what that was about?"

"I don't like him."

"Yeah, I picked up on that. But *why?*"

"I just..." Mike shook himself from head to toe, his shoulders unlocking, his anger draining away at last. But with it gone, his gaze became lost. He stood there staring at nothing, as though he'd dreamed the outburst and now the details were slipping away.

"I don't want him here. He doesn't belong. Not after what he did."

"What he... Bear, what're you talking about? Did this kid like, key your car in a past life or something?"

"No."

"Do you know him?"

"I..." For all the world, his husband looked like he needed to say "yes" but the conviction wouldn't come.

"Okay, bear... Breathe," Eric continued, putting a much gentler hand on his arm.

"I don't... I just don't..."

"Just take a breath, all right? The whole overprotective father thing is cute but you can't go around murdering every kid that turns up on our front porch."

"Do... Do *you* like him?"

"I don't *know* him, bear, but for first impressions, he seemed okay. Besides, we've been here for two weeks and the only person I've talked to for more than five minutes is the waitress at the diner. Of all the guys she could've met, at least this one's polite."

"I don't... I don't like him," he said again, but his face drawn and weary, as if the anger had been the only thing holding him up. "He doesn't belong."

"Okay, okay," Eric said , brushing his fingers along Mike's temple, cupping his cheek. " Bear, why don't you go lie down for a while? It'll be a bit before dinner. I promise, I'll wake you when it's ready."

Without saying a word, Mike turned away. By the time he was halfway up the stairs, he was grunting with effort and leaning on the banister like a crutch.

Eric massaged his face with both hands and tried to wipe the stress away. He hated how Mike looked almost as much as he hated the way he'd treated Emily. He knew at some point he'd have to apologize, but if Emily had let fly at Mike, it would've turned into a screaming fest they'd all have regretted.

With everyone gone, the house was as quiet as it ever got, the only sounds the click of Mike's door and Emily and Iris laughing somewhere just above Eric's head. He wanted to write everything off as an exhausted father looking out for his baby girl, but it was only one of an ever-increasing list of strange things he'd encountered over the last two weeks.

With a house this large and so much land, he never thought for a second that Iris *wouldn't* take off like a cannonball. But of the two of them, it was Emily who left every morning, all but forcing her bike into town while Iris spent most of her time in her room.

A deep and exhausted part of Eric wanted to worry but had nothing to go on. Every time he saw his little conqueror she was breathless and happy and so dusty Eric wanted to Swiffer the living hell out of her.

Weirdest of all though was Mike, a man who never stopped moving. Every time Eric turned around, he found Mike weeding, cleaning, or carrying some new bit of furniture up the stairs. Before the sea chest it was a teak side table, the sort of thing meant for teatime and snack cakes, not for real people who made awful messes. It had taken all of one look for Eric to hate the thing, and each successive piece Mike dredged up only served to remind him that *they* didn't belong. That this house had a history and expectations and it would mold them to it whether they liked it or not.

Unable to do anything about the sea chest, Eric rolled up his sleeves and stepped over to the mantle. Taking a firm hold of the portrait, he locked eyes with the matriarch and it was a fight not to recoil, as though the old woman were a stray dog or a loud bang that rattled the windows. Gritting his teeth, Eric pulled the thing off the wall, the weight of it almost throwing him off balance. Recovering with a huff, he carried the hideous thing down the hall and tucked it into the closet.

"Ugh," he said at last, wiping his hands on his jeans, as though the portrait left an oily film behind. Slamming the door behind him helped to ease some of the worries in his mind. . It took only a few minutes of searching to find one of his own paintings to take its place. It wasn't a perfect fit but it was one of his favorites, a road trip they'd taken to Hershey Park, each of them captured as a family of penguins cheering as they zipped down a rollercoaster.

With a deep sigh, Eric let his head fall back, feeling the little cracks of tension give in the base of his neck. He hummed to himself as he began to fix dinner, the tune becoming a prayer that they would all be in much better spirits when the time came to eat it.

9
ME

DAMN HIM. DAMN THAT boy. Oh, how I wished I could've blamed him for everything. Left all the blood to come up to his machinations. But no. Much as I hated to admit it, I had to blame myself. There could be no other explanation. I let my attention drift for one moment, allowed anger to cloud my judgment, and a Cruel One slithered his way in.

It'd been years since I'd seen him but he could be no one else. The boy who stuck like a parasite to Emily was just the same as every bastard child who visited me. Scrawny and unfinished, covering their inadequacy as they pelted me with rocks and sticks.

And then here he was. Making eyes at Emily, his smile like a broken limb that never mended. I rotted at the heart to see him again. Yearned for my family to drive him off like an intruder, like the *monster* I knew him to be.

But I'd poured too much anger into Michael, primed him like a bomb until even Eric feared his explosion. He didn't have my history with the Cruel One. He didn't know how much I'd suffered because of him and others like him. Oh, there'd been so many others.

But I couldn't let my frustrations get the better of me. I needed to be more like the spiders who spun their webs in my eaves every year. They didn't scavenge. They never fretted. Instead, they waited. Their traps set, their patience infinite, even as a hunger beat away within them. Spiders knew an opportunity would present itself. And when it did, the Cruel One would know nothing but thrashing limbs and teeth.

I may have suffered because of him, but what damage he'd done had been mended. My eyes were clear, my skin pristine, my bones as strong as the ground beneath them. I was whole again. And he would pay for everything he did to me.

10
ERIC

THE COLORS WOULDN'T COME together. That was how he thought of it. Like his head and his hand had different ideas and neither was listening to the other. Scraping jagged fingernails through his scalp, Eric hoped to feed some good, creative vibes back into his skull. Never before had a project given him so much trouble, which was a shame, because this was his first real moment alone in weeks.

Mike left over an hour ago, off on another supply run. His third of the week. While Emily and Iris were in the front yard playing what Eric was sure was a super important game Iris made up five minutes before. With all the doors shut and the central air running, Eric couldn't even hear them, though he made a point of glancing out the window every few minutes. A part of him, never all that far away, told him he should feel guilty for not checking on his girls more often, and though he did his best not to listen to it, staring at a blank stretch of canvas which did nothing but stare back, was not exactly productive.

Tired of guilt, but unable to escape it, Eric turned his back on the canvas and marched down to the kitchen. Pausing just long enough to refresh his coffee, he looked toward the front of the house but shook his head with a frustrated sigh.

Between his problems with Mike, this uncomfortable house, and his mother's grating voice stuck in his head, Eric was in no mood for company, much as he loved his daughters like the breath in his lungs. Strangling that persistent feeling of guilt , he threw open the back door and stomped his way out onto the grass.

The heat of the day consumed him just past the steps, but he didn't mind. It was at least a sensation he was prepared for. Up until today, he'd thought his new studio would be something he could grow into. Somewhere quiet and full of light where his art could thrive, which was all he'd ever really wanted. But as he strode across the wide, almost neon green lawn, he admitted the truth—if only to himself. He dreaded walking down the hall. It was a problem he couldn't wrap his mind around but he also couldn't put it aside.

He got about a hundred feet away from the house, then stopped, his paint stained shoes lost in the ankle high grass. Civilization may have been behind him, but right in front was nothing but weeds and a forest. Hip high fronds of crab grass swayed lazily in the breeze, while brown-bodied elms and copper beech trees all but crashed into each other.

Relaxing his eyes, Eric could imagine what this place must've been like before Dierdre planted her own house-shaped, personal flag. Woods running riot, flowers in crimson, peach, and gold, the scent of old earth mixed with the brightness of saplings growing. It was such a pretty picture to conjure up, and the land might've stayed that way for years if Dierdre hadn't decided *this* was the place she wanted to be seen.

With a sad sigh, Eric kept walking, not really conscious of where he was going until he tripped over a small patch of ground he'd mistaken for an aborted garden.

The plot was close to two hundred feet away from the house, which made sense, since Eric doubted even Deirdre would have wanted to see a cemetery just outside her bedroom window.

Here, the grass grew tall and unruly, the fronds brushing Eric's fingertips. He made a mental note to have it cut back. The last thing he needed was for Iris to come home with ticks buried in her skin. There was no fence bordering the plot or even a sign to mark it, and as Eric dropped to one knee he hissed as something jagged dug into his leg. Brushing away the grass he found a broken piece of headstone with roots growing up through the cracks at the edges. No name could be read and even making out the dates was a stretch.

As he picked his way along , Eric found a song playing in the back of his head. One so quiet he almost missed it, but as his thoughts played it back again, the song grew louder and a rueful smile played at the corners of his lips. It might not have been respectful, in fact it bordered on blasphemy, but as his thoughts about money and the house and the people who built it coalesced, he let the song come crashing out of his mouth like cold water poured onto a dish straight from the oven.

Oh Lord, won't you buy me a Mercedes Benz.

My friends all drive Porches, I must make amends.

Worked hard all my life, no help from my friends.

Oh Lord, won't you buy me...a Mercedes Bennnnnzzz!

He laughed as he stretched the last word out, the strange bit of happiness enough to make him keep going. "Thank you, thank you! I'll be here until I'm dead!"

He found the next grave with the toe of his shoe. Its once innocent cherub reduced to half a face and the name sandblasted away. He dug through the abandonment for ten more minutes but found nothing except a growing sense of anger and contempt. Gritting his teeth, he looked back at the house, wanting to spit, unable to fathom anyone, let alone a whole family, dedicating themselves to appearances so much that they neglected their own graves in the end.

Eric kicked his way through the weeds one last time and then sneered as a name appeared, of course much more intact than the rest. Above Deirdre's name sat an angel, its eyes gone black from the flowers that had died within them. Eric checked the date and had to resist the urge to kick the woman's final resting place. Despite how hateful Dierdre had been, she'd lived to a ripe old age. But it was the words etched in a grand, calligraphic script below which stayed with Eric the most. *I will always be with you*, it read, and Eric, fed up with decay and stupidity, tromped his way out of that dry, wretched place, in search of a tall glass of ice water.

He was halfway to the door when a glinting movement just up the road caught his attention. Shielding his eyes, he smiled as Jason pedaled toward them. Hey may have been scared of the place but he was coming all the same, and Eric couldn't decide whether that made him foolish or brave or both.

Maybe he's just young, he thought and grinned even wider as he heard Emily shout *"Hi!"* from clear across the yard. With a quick step, Eric swept through the house, stopping only long enough to down half a glass of water and then refill. It couldn't have been more than a minute or two before he stepped out onto the porch but judging by the way Emily and Jason smiled at each other, it had been enough.

Off to one side, Iris sat in the grass with her sword across her knees. Her eyes jumped from her sister to Jason and back again before landing on Eric.

"Papa, is that an invader?" she asked, pointing her dimpled chin at Jason.

"Iris!" Emily countered, somehow both shouting and hissing her sister's name at the same time.

"No, sweetie," Eric replied, not even bothering to stifle a laugh. "That's not an invader. That's Emily's *special friend*."

"*Papa!*"

"And he's staying for lunch," Eric continued, as though his eldest hadn't spoken.

"I... I am?" Jason stuttered, his face glowing vermilion but damn if he didn't stand his ground. "I uh...just came over to return the book I borrowed."

"That's a *long* way to go," Eric said, still smiling.

For once, it was Emily who put herself in the middle. She caught Jason's eye, her own face a riot of colors, but her voice was steady.

"You don't have to stay for lunch," she said.

"Um... Okay."

"Unless..." Emily's voice dropped an octave.

"Yeah?" Jason asked in the key of youthful hope.

"Unless you, y'know *want* to stay for lunch."

"Um, yeah," he answered with rising happiness. "I mean, I'm kinda hungry. My mom is taking care of my grandma today so our fridge is kinda..."

"Bare?" Emily finished and Eric choked at the way they both colored then. Had he just started something he'd regret later? Maybe. But for now the moment was too good to pass up.

"Then it's settled," he said, trying to break up the awkwardness but Emily wasn't done yet.

"Is it settled with dad?" she asked and even Eric had to pause with that one.

It should have been a simple question, but Eric couldn't miss the way Emily glanced around or the relief he saw on his daughter's face that Mike wasn't home. He'd been gone a while and might be home at any time but...

"It'll be fine," Eric said , giving Jason a firm nod. "Do you like tuna?" This he asked with faux gravity, hoping to lighten the mood though he couldn't help but notice the way Jason hesitated before replying.

"Yeah, I do. Thank you." he said.

"Then it really is settled." Eric ushered the three of them into the house, thankful that no one else asked him a question he didn't have an answer to.

Plugging in the toaster, he sat the kids down at the kitchen table and rummaged until he had everything he needed.

"Okay everyone! Pick your poison. What kind of chips do you want?"

"Ranch!" Iris the conqueror demanded.

Eric stayed where he was, head cocked, eyes narrowing.

"Please!" came a moment later.

"That's better," Eric replied.

Not in the mood to deal with washing dishes, Eric made a bee-line to the closet for paper plates and napkins. But the moment he opened the door, Portrait Dierdre and the rest of the Miller Clan came falling out, the heavy gilt frame scratching his thigh before hitting the floor with a *whump*.

"Damn it!" he cried, giving the ugly thing a good kick, which sent it sliding across the floor.

"Papa? Are you okay?" Iris asked, brandishing her sword while also half hiding behind her chair.

"Yes, sweetie. I'm fine," Eric replied, unable to keep the anger out of his voice. Rather than give the frame another kick, he took a deep breath and held it, letting the balloon of air in his belly push any choice words out through the bones of his chest.

By the time he let the breath out, he was no less angry, but a little more in control than before.

He looked back at the kids to find Jason had risen out of his seat like he meant to offer help but wasn't sure how to get the words out. The gesture was worth a small smile.

"I'm fine, really. Sorry, it just caught me off guard." With a shake of his head, Eric picked up the frame. From within, Deirdre's expression appeared even more imperious than before. Her cold, expansive gaze practically screaming, *You thought you won, but here I am.*

Fighting the urge to flip Dierdre the bird, Eric leaned the thing against the wall and then snatched up plates and napkins.

"What is *that*?" Emily asked.

Eric looked back but took a second to appreciate the sight before answering. All three kids sat with their backs to the big bay window, the day framing them with warm yellow light. Eric blinked, filing the image away for another painting on a better day.

"Your father's idea of fine art," he grumbled, taking out his frustrations on the can opener and a can of tuna.

Emily studied the portrait and then glanced at Eric with one eyebrow raised. "This isn't gonna be like the leg lamp in *A Christmas Story*, is it? You and Dad going to war while Iris and me look on in shame?"

Eric chuckled, the sound good enough to push out the dark thoughts gumming up his head. "Your dad and I are not going to war," he said, before smirking at his daughter . "But if we ever did, he'd *lose*. I mean, look at this thing! Can you believe it?" In the midst of draining the tuna, Eric pointed at the frame with a wet paper towel. "I mean, c'mon. Who could love someone—some*thing*—like this?"

Emily opened her mouth to reply but it was Jason who got there first.

"Yeah, everybody hated that lady."

Surprised, Eric turned to find him, watched his gaze skitter between Eric and Emily, his cheeks pinking once again.

"Sorry," he said , wiping his mouth with the back of his hand.

"No, no, it's okay. Do you... Do you know who this is?" Eric tapped the frame with a finger, just over Dierdre's dominating head.

Jason rolled his shoulders and leaned forward, appearing happy to talk about a bit of local history.

"My grandma used to call her Old Lady Horror," he said, while from somewhere nearby pipes groaned. Jason jumped as though his words had caused offense, but Eric snickered.

"Yeah, she looks like a real charmer. Did your grandmother know her?"

"Not really. Nobody did. I mean, she did the washing for the family, but the Old Lady never really left the house."

Emily perked up at that. "Oooh, so was she like, the town recluse or something? The town boogey...lady?"

"Bitch," Eric offered, surprised at his own language but not regretting the word. It fit too well.

"The boogeybitch!" Emily crowed. "That's awesome! I like it!"

Jason waggled one hand in an either-or motion. "To hear my grandma tell it, yeah she kind of was. She's supposed to be buried up here somewhere, along with the rest of the family."

Eric took a large baking sheet out of the cabinet, set out slices of bread and covered each with a slice of Swiss cheese. He tried to make it sound casual as she asked, "What were they like? The family, I mean."

Jason shrugged. "Weird, I guess. Grandma said they were all off their rockers. The Old Lady built the place and then never left. Like, ever. She said one of the daughters would bring the laundry by once a week. Millicent, that was her name."

He pointed to the youngest in the picture, she with the straight back and imperious expression, the one the mother had gotten her claws into early.

"How'd they go grocery shopping?" Emily asked, looking perplexed. "Did they have Peapod back in the day?"

Jason smiled and shook his head. "Nah. She'd just send the daughters to pick up whatever they needed. Only person I know who even talked to her was my grandpa."

"Oh, yeah? What was he?" Eric asked. "A former gentleman caller?"

"Huh?"

Emily nudged him. "Old boyfriend."

"Oh. Oh, *ew*, no! No way. He only talked to her like one time and that was just cause of..." He paused and looked away as though unsure how to continue or even if he should.

"It's okay, go on," Eric said.

"Yeah," Emily chimed in. "We love juicy bits of madness in this house."

Emboldened, Jason straightened up and cleared his throat. "My grandpa used to own this furniture store in town, right? Had it for, like, years."

"Is your grandfather the one I have to thank for all the ugly crap in my basement?" Eric asked with a smirk.

Jason laughed and shook his head. "Nah, the Old Lady never really bought anything from him, except this one time. Grandma *did* say it was cause Grandpa didn't stock anything ugly enough for them."

Eric smiled. "I've got a feeling I'd like your grandmother."

"Me too," Emily said, and if Jason smiled at Eric's compliment, he *glowed* at Emily's.

"So, um, anyway," he continued still blushing, "one night, Grandpa got a delivery of this really nice cabinet, like *super* high end. He takes one look at it and figures the Old Lady might like it, but it's way too late to call. So he puts the thing in the display window for the night and says he'll talk to her in the morning."

"Makes sense," Eric said, mixing together mayo, garlic powder, onion powder, and lemon juice.

"Yeah, yeah, but see what he *didn't* know,"—Jason was grinning, possessed by the story now—" was Millicent was already in town running errands when she happened to walk by the store. Grandma and Grandpa had just climbed into bed when they heard this *giant* crash from downstairs. They come running to find the display window's busted and the cabinet's gone."

"Oh my god," Eric said.

"Dude!" Emily barked, excited.

"I know, right? But that's not the weirdest thing. One of the neighbors across the street saw the whole thing. She said Millicent didn't even use, like, a rock or anything , just crashed right through the window, like *boom*, face first. When the cops picked her up a few blocks away, she was covered in blood and *still* trying to drag the cabinet up to the house."

"Holy crap!" Iris burst out.

"Did your grandpa press charges?" Eric asked.

"Oh, like crazy. Grandma wanted to get a restraining order against the whole family."

"And did she?"

"No, but it wasn't for lack of trying."

Eric decided to bring Jason's grandmother a really good bottle of wine if they ever got together.

The four of them laughed and it was a comforting sound. Jason's voice melded well with theirs, making Eric imagine it could be there for a while.

"So anyway," Jason said, continuing "the day after Millicent got out of the hospital, Grandpa got a call from the Old Lady. He figured she wanted to talk about paying for the damage. No. She wanted to talk about the cabinet. She said Millicent wouldn't shut up about it and if he still had it she'd like him to sell."

"Oh my god," Eric said again, fighting the urge to let his face fall into his hands.

"Did he sell it to her?" Emily pressed, now shoulder to shoulder with Jason.

"No way," Jason replied, his eyes locked on her. "He told her it got damaged and he had to send it back. Then he stashed it in our attic. We still have it. My mom hides our Christmas presents in it every year."

"I'd have sold it to her," Eric declared, squaring his shoulders and lifting his chin.

"Really?" the three of them asked, even Iris looked at him cockeyed.

"Sure," he said smiling. "For three times the price."

That got the three of them laughing, but it was Emily who recovered first. "Pffft, you'd have told her to go to hell," she said. "*Dad* would've sold it to her for three times the price."

Knowing she was right, Eric nodded. "True."

The sound of their dying laugher helped to break up the last bit of tension in Eric's belly. From somewhere nearby, the house let out an ominous creak, but they ignored it, lost in the sound of the oven timer going off. They all sighed as the room filled with the smell of warm bread and melted cheese.

Slathering on a thick serving of tuna for each of them, they sat around the table and shared three different bags of chips. The sun baked them with a pleasant, welcoming heat as they traded jabs and stories. Smiling, Eric knew that amid all the laughter and light, when he next stepped into his studio, it would be to paint with the darkest colors imaginable and screw if it made sense.

With his decision made, he felt better than he had in days. Even as Emily and Iris flung chips at each other, he couldn't bring himself to care about the mess. Anything could be cleaned up and besides, the house, for all its gaudy, self-important grandeur, could do with getting a little messy.

11
ME

I WOULD NEVER FORGIVE them. Not ever. Little Iris I might forgive in time, but the rest... I had a history of blood and sacrifice in me, and it would not be disrespected. They should have known better.

They sat around the table my first family had bled for and they let the Cruel Boy spread his lies. But while what came next might have been born from anger, I felt regret more than anything else. Regret that I might lose them if I didn't take drastic steps.

I watched Eric deposit Mother in the hall closet but made a note to have Michael return her later. She deserved pride of place. If ever I shined, it was because of her. Michael may have restored me, but she gave me life and bid me feed.

And as the four of them cleared lunch away, I knew one thing for certain. I would do everything I could to protect my family. No matter what it cost them in the end.

It wasn't long before Iris came to me like she always did, leaping up the stairs, sword in hand, a smile on her angelic face.

With extra chips crunching about in her pockets, she slid across the floor on her knees, stopping before the panel I'd shown her weeks ago. Tucked into the corner of the closet, Iris had taken to keeping a small nest of 'supplies'. A can of soda, a bag of rainbow-colored worms, and handfuls of chalk in every shade. Even with my first family, my insides had never been so vibrant, so colorful. My goodness, I loved her too much.

Grabbing her supplies , she pulled aside the panel and shuffled through. Her denim overalls took the brunt of the dust and dirt that populated my hidden spaces, but the brush of her fingers sent chills straight through my bones. She'd made a home inside of me cobbled together from blankets scrounged out of several rooms. It was a good place, one where I could watch over her easily. Because I was the only one who could.

She drew castles inside of me. Planets, warriors, comets, great glowing suns. But for as much as she giggled, it wasn't long before she started to yawn and then curled up into a ball atop her blankets. I filled myself with a slow, satisfying heat and muffled the sounds of the outside world, sealing her up like a precious jewel. She needed time away. Time to appreciate what I could give her. How safe and happy she would be with me.

I watched those blessed eyes flick through dreams and then I dreamed along with her. I fantasized about her growing up, of Michael passing his duties onto her. The joys I'd show her one day. Picking out the finest furniture, dressing properly, the sweet, satisfied ache that comes from years of service. I mapped out the life I'd build for her. She would be so happy. She *belonged* with me. I just had to keep her safe until then.

12

ERIC

HE WORKED IN BLACK, gray, red, and green. Each of them so dark they absorbed the light, drawing it in the way winter will eat up a fire's heat. He laid each color with a steady hand as he moved across the canvas, marveling at how different they became the further they got from the storm.

The closer he came to the house, the more the colors turned something malignant. His gray solidified into stone, old, and long buried, his black the deep shadows and cracks between them. His green was rot with its tendrils like a root structure beneath the house. And his red... His red he didn't know what it was yet, even as he daubed it on with his smallest brush. Stepping back, he though they looked like candle flames burning beneath the house.

As he wiped a hand across his forehead, he glanced at the clock. "Dammit."

He should've had dinner started ten minutes ago. Cleaning his brushes, he gave his painting a onceover, happy to see how close to the end he was. With the block gone, he'd flown across the canvas, leaving only the cutouts yet to be filled in.

He'd already decided to leave the house blank, only its edges blurred by the colors surrounding it. He did this not because the house didn't matter but because, in his mind, it was more like window dressing, like the way gaudy jewelry could hide the horrific person who wore it.

Despite the fact that it was the darkest picture he'd ever created, Eric was surprised at how happy he felt. Like so many of his portraits, it helped him frame his thoughts and, staring at the house, it wasn't only his thoughts but his actions which coalesced around it. Mike had gone on about the few years they would spend here, but deep down Eric knew. There would be no few years here. If he had anything to say about it, there wouldn't even be one.

He had no illusions about the *fight* this would be. After everything Mike had put into this place, he wouldn't want to leave. But they had to and no matter what, Eric would make him see that. For the sake of all of them, Mike had to see that this place was...thinking about his distracted face, Eric realized how *thin* Mike was becoming, the picture on him on their nightstand looked like the younger, healthier version of the man Eric now shared a bed with.

The skin of his face was tight to his skull, the veins in his hands more prominent as the flesh receded, revealing what lay beneath.

Shaking his head, Eric tore his eyes away from the house and turned to his happy little family, who all had no idea what was waiting for them. Like the house, he meant to leave them blank, but as he studied their faces, something new scratched away.

On instinct, he rummaged through his paints, picking out a can he hadn't opened yet. Prying off the lid, he dipped his smallest brush and then held it a few inches away from the canvas. The color wasn't one he used often. It couldn't even be called a color, really. Titanium white wasn't meant to be dabbed or brushed; it was a filler. Something artists spread across their canvas to give the *real* colors something to cling to.

But for as true as the color felt right then, still he hesitated, not liking what he wanted to do, though it felt as faithful to real life as everything else he painted. Eric stood still for several seconds while the clocked ticked away, reminding him how it would be eight o'clock before they all ate dinner if he didn't move his ass.

Sick of pausing, Eric reached out and, with a deft flick, blotted out a section of canvas so small it was hard to believe it mattered. But staring at it from inches away, he knew it revealed a truth more impactful than anything else. Amidst all the colors, his reds and grays and blacks and greens, one figure no longer had a face. It sat in the front seat of the cartoon car, its features obliterated, leading its family toward whatever awaited them at the end.

Slipping out of his studio, Eric shuffled down the hall, his head full of a quiet sadness. Through Emily's door, music drifted, something loud and peppy that had Eric smiling as he heard the floorboards creak. He easily imagined his daughter dancing before the mirror just like he had, just like every once-upon-a-time kid did in their day.

He'd been about to hustle down the stairs to make dinner, but the lack of light coming from Iris's room pulled him up short.

It was both too late and too early for his perpetual motion device to be sleeping.

Peeking in, the room was dark, empty, strangely cold, as though the heat had given out here but nowhere else.

"Iris?" Eric called, and much like weeks ago, no reply came. Only this time, Eric found it harder to fight against the tightness in his belly. Back then, the lights had been on, the sun just starting to pour through the windows. There'd been the feeling he'd missed Iris by only a few seconds and, if he listened, he might've heard the *thump-thump-thump* of her feet rumbling up behind him. But right then, the room sat unmoved, as though no one had been there for days.

"Iris?" he called again, a little more strident than before. "Iris, where are you?"

That horrible, squiggly feeling, the one he'd fought down weeks ago, returned again. Stronger, more deeply set, the sensation twist-ed up his insides as though it had hands of concrete. Eric hated how raspy his voice became the more he went on. "Iris! Talk to me! *Iris!*"

Eric launched his daughter's name into the depths of the house but the house gave him nothing back. The peppy music in Emily's room died as his eldest ripped the door open. She stared at Eric with a rising panic, her lips twisted in fear.

"Papa?" she asked in such a hopeful way it broke Eric's heart. Eric looked back at her and the look was enough. Tears welled in Emily's eyes.

"Iris?" they called together, each of them getting louder by the minute.

"Olly-olly oxen-free!" Emily cried, fighting to smile. "Time to come out!"

Again, the house gave them nothing.

They searched the place from top to bottom. In the basement they shoved aside hideous furniture and tore up old sheets. Always together, never alone.

"Iris?" Emily pleaded.

"Sweetheart?" Eric countered.

Not a sound.

They ran out into the yard and shouted. Their voices hitting the town line and beyond.

Mike came home and added his voice to theirs. It sounded hollow but Eric didn't hold it against him. Not then. Together, they yelled so loud it hurt.

And nothing.

They searched everywhere one more time. And then they did it again.

Hours passed. The day darkened.

Eric grew hoarse as he screamed.

13

ME

I WATCHED THEM RUN but allowed Iris to go on dreaming. She was too precious to let go of yet. Oh, my dear Iris. She made the most wonderful sounds in her sleep. I could have listened to her for ages, but nothing good ever lasts.

My new family scoured me for hours and while I worried they might do some permanent damage, my dear Michael was there for me as always. Even as Eric and Emily threw open doors and dumped out cupboards, Michael followed close behind. He shut each door with a careful hand and made sure the cupboards weren't scratched. He stared in indignation at a spill of flour and I could see him marking it clearly in his head. A map of things to be cleaned later. My goodness, I loved that man. But Michael's care for me almost brought things to a head with Eric, it must be said.

Eric came streaming out of the pantry, wide-eyed and sweating, to find Michael scrubbing a scuff mark out of the floor.

"What are you *doing*?" he barked and I could all but hear Michael's reply before he said anything. It would have been cogent and reasonable too. A cool, calm, litany of my importance, one that spoke to the quality of wood, the effort and expense, and the way little imperfections had of always piling up. But even as Michael opened his mouth, I blew a chill wind across his thoughts, tamping down the flames rather than scattering sparks.

I made him hesitate and though I knew what he'd been doing was right, there was a time for peace, and a time to fight and I was more than old enough to know the difference.

"Sorry," he said, his thoughts nuzzling against me like a kitten in need of reassurance. "I just... I don't know what to do. Where do we look next?"

Eric's face, which had been so hot and taut that he looked ready to howl, softened as tears sprang to his eyes. With a shaking step, he crossed to Michael and took his hand. "I don't know either, but..."

There was a light tromping on the basement stairs, the sound of Emily making her way up. For a moment, Eric's face contorted in hope, the porchlight of his thoughts ready to welcome all wayward children home.

But the version of Emily who slouched her way up into the light, looked both ready to cry and fall asleep at the same time. Her clothes were dusty, her hair disheveled, the mark of someone who'd truly gone looking but gained nothing in return.

"Any luck?" Eric asked, the hope in him still struggling for life.

Emily shook her head. "Where could she be?" she cried, her thin chest heaving, her voice on the edge of sobbing. I felt for her, I truly did. But there was a lesson to be taught here and we were all in far too deep to stop yet.

"She's hiding somewhere, she's gotta be," Michael said, throwing up his hands, only to let them slap against his thighs.

"This isn't hide and seek, Mike," Eric replied, scraping ten ragged fingernails through his unwashed hair.

Michael snorted. "Maybe not for us. But for her…"

"Jesus, dad!" Emily spat. "Do you, like, not know her at all?"

Emily squared up against Michael, and the flames, oh how they leaped in him then. Great fiery tongues that could've burned whole forests down and I almost laughed at the way Emily stilled, her weight balanced onto the balls of her feet. She looked ready to run but was too young to know that wasn't an option. Fear was a good thing more often than not. A sign of respect to those who could take everything from her, and she owed it Michael, if for no other reason than because he hadn't written her future yet. But it would be written here soon, with *me*.

So as Emily stood before her father and paled, her heels *tap-tap-tapping* against my floor, I wish I could've stretched that moment, made it indelible like a mark she carried forever. But as so often happened in those days, Eric interrupted, and there was a crust of dried spit in the corner of his mouth as he growled.

"*This isn't helping.*"

I allowed Michael a small smirk as he stared at Emily. "Listen to your papa, kid. Now's not the time to get grounded."

I don't have words for the sound Eric made then.

"That's not what I mean!" he cried, smacking Michael hard on the shoulder. Eric's bitter, angry eyes bored into their confused faces. With his hands balled into fists, he took a deep breath, his voice just on the cusp of bestial howls.

"Emily's right, Mike," he said, tying down each word as though afraid they might take off running. "Iris is not the kind of kid to pull pranks. She's *never* been that kind of kid. She's still here, stuck somewhere, which means you two glaring at each other is doing *fuck all to help with that!*"

It was moments like this which made me like Eric all over again. How I wished he weren't so stubborn, so blind to all we could've accomplished. He could've been a kind of patriarch in his own right. But...

"We've already searched everywhere twice," Michael said, cracking his neck. "So either she's invisible or all of us are blind."

"I'm telling you, she's here!" Eric insisted with all the desperation of someone willing to believe a lie.

They couldn't have understood, not even Michael really. They couldn't have known what it took to keep Iris quiet. To muffle the sounds of the world until they were like a river heard over a distant hill.

But it was my job to school them. To make them understand what love costs and how many sacrifices perfection required. I didn't do this without remorse, but rather with a hard-edged regret for as much as I loved the sounds Iris made, I couldn't keep her hidden forever.

It was only a matter of time before she woke, her little belly rumbling, fingers grasping for her sword. So as Eric led the others up the stairs one more time, it wasn't a coincidence that Iris stirred then. I believed in that even less than I believed in providence. No, after all my years, I knew there was no such thing as fate, only patience and good timing. And as far as providence went... Well, when it came to my family...I was the only providence within reach.

As they stomped their way up the stairs, I let their noises intrude. Iris hadn't even sat up before she started coughing. All my little secrets lived in places of dust.

"Did you hear that?" Eric asked, stopping so fast Emily collided with him.

"I didn't hear anything," Michael replied, and it took everything I had not to let him sound too flippant or worse yet...bored.

"I know I heard something!" Eric insisted. "Emily?" he asked, looking at his daughter to be his calvary.

"I... I don't..." Emily hedged, too unsure to answer.

Michael shook his head. "Scribble, she's not here."

"She has to be!" Eric roared, past caring how he sounded. "Iris! Sweetheart?"

Michael took Eric's arm, tried to pull him back down the stairs. "Scrib, why don't we check in the basement?"

"We already looked there! *Twice!*"

Michael groaned. "That's just what I said before! Are you seriously going to—"

"Will both of you shut up?" Emily yowled, having found her voice at last. "Iris! Come on, Iris! Where are you?"

"This is pointless," Michael groused. "Let's just head back down the stairs and—"

"Papa?"

Everyone stopped, each of them all but tripping over the others. Iris's voice was groggy and her hair was full of cobwebs.

"Tell... Tell me you heard that," Eric gasped, his eyes flicking this way and that, hands like fishhooks ready to haul his baby to shore.

"Somebody tell me they heard that!" he cried again, neither his husband nor his daughter ready to say one way or the other.

"Iris?" Eric called one last time.

Within me, Iris rubbed her eyes, then rubbed them again as the dust crept its way beneath her lids.

"Papa? Ow, Papa what..." she whined.

"*Baby, I'm here!*" Eric roared.

"I heard it too!" Emily cried.

Michael shook his head. "I can't believe..."

All three of them spoke at once as Iris scurried forward, her knees eradicating the art she'd created hours before.

"Where's it coming from?" Eric pleaded.

"I don't know!"

"Iris! Where are you?"

"I'm here!" Iris yelled. It wasn't far to the entrance, just a short crawl, but I couldn't let her go then. The lesson was not yet finished and I needed it to hurt if any of them were going to get better.

"I'm right..." Iris's small, soft hands pawed at the panel, her face screwing up in confusion as it refused to budge. She would have been adorable were it not for the tears. "Papa, it won't open!"

In the past I'd always helped her, made sure the wood gave way with ease. But that night she was like a bunny trying to shift a boulder, one that blocked all the light and life in the world.

She groaned, her little chest hitching, her breath coming in hot streaks.

"Papa? Papa, I need *help*!"

"We're coming! We're coming, sweetie!" Eric cried. "But I need you to tell me where you are!"

Little Iris rubbed her precious eyes, which only made the pain that much worse.

"*Papa!*"

"I think it's coming from her room," Emily said, taking a hesitant step forward.

"It can't be," Michael replied, reaching for her. "We checked there three times already."

Eric didn't bother to argue, just took off running down the hall. At Iris's door, he skidded, his fingers gouging out long swathes of my skin. I couldn't blame him. Not really. It may have hurt, but I'd have Michael fix it later, once the dust had settled.

In the center of Iris's room, Eric stopped, his feet pointed north, his hands east and west, and his head trying to cover every point of the compass at once.

"Iris?" he called.

Michael and Emily followed. Michael took one look around and shook his head. " Scrib, she's not—"

"PAPA!"

Eric's directionless body came together almost fast enough to break bones. All three of my family turned to stare at the closet, but it was Eric who made it there first.

One might think I would've let go then, allowed them to have their happy reunion. But even here, the lesson was not finished. Eric needed to grunt and fight, to rip nails out by the root before I could relent.

Blood, yes. There was blood and tears because there had to be. The best lessons are always the most painful.

By the time they took the panel away, Iris's beautiful face was a mask of dust, her soft voice broken from crying. I regretted this, I did, but I would have done it all over again, because the lesson was finally finished. Or so I thought.

The theatrics I expected. Sweet Iris babbling about her ordeal, and the hugs and tears which followed. It didn't even take that much to squeeze a tear out of Michael. He and I were growing closer by the day. Eric bundled up Iris and carried her downstairs, fed and fussed over her for so long that I thought they'd all fall asleep, the whole family encamped around the dinner table until morning. But eventually fear siphoned out and Iris's head began to droop in her papa's lap.

It amazed me that Eric had the strength to carry her back upstairs, but he did it without complaint. Together, he and Michael tucked Iris into their own bed, my dear one's small body like a rowboat lost in a blanket sea.

With a trembling hand, Eric waved Michael out and then tiptoed into the hallway. Michael returned to the kitchen, but Emily hovered nearby, looking so tired she could've fallen asleep if she leaned against me for too long. Eric walked her to her room and somehow found the strength to wait until she was asleep before leaving again.

Out in the hall, Eric's steps were slow and unsteady, the trials of the day costing him just to remain upright. I half expected him to retreat to his own room, but even here, he surprised me. At the top of the stairs, he leaned against the banister but made no move to head down. Instead, he turned and looked back, his eyes fixing on the door to Iris's room.

Maybe it was instinct, or perhaps Iris's talk of what 'the house' did to her. But whatever the reason, Eric stopped at his daughter's door and listened, as though afraid some great beast were snuffling about in the shadows. After a moment, he strode over to the panel, picked at it with his injured hand and then grabbed a ruler out of one of Iris's drawers.

His makeshift crowbar might have been cheap, but it was effective, nonetheless. Wedging it between the wood, he pried at my inner workings until the panel gave way.

I could have resisted him, it's true. Made him fight until he lost another nail or worse, but I didn't because there was still a lesson to be taught here. One I hadn't expected. So, I let him crawl in, allowed his adult body to invade Iris's imaginary kingdom, and as he shuffled in, his head tucked low, arms tight to his sides, I wanted to laugh. He was thinking of a child's world, afraid of cracking his head on beams or bumping into corners that didn't exist. It wasn't until he stood up, stretched out those arms and caught nothing but air, that he began to understand.

It was the way his breathing changed that struck me the most. A fast, ragged, fearful panting, which wheezed up from the bottom of his lungs, and oh...the look on his face. He knew me then in a way even Michael did not, and it was perfect because he not only saw the true length and breadth of me, he witnessed the little improvements Mother had made over the years.

The patches she'd cut, the little holes she'd bored to keep an eye on her children. Eric touched them all with trembling fingers and I could see it in his dusty face. The knowledge and possibility. The instant when he knew exactly how prepared I was for them. What safe and ordered and fulfilling lives they might lead, with me watching over them.

Oh, it would be wonderful, oh yes. I would *make* it wonderful for them.

14
ERIC

WELL PAST MIDNIGHT, ERIC and Mike sat in the kitchen and said nothing, the silence like a gulf between them, almost too distant to shout across. Eric couldn't remember the last time he'd been this wrung out. His eyes burned, his head felt heavy and though his stomach was wracked by hunger pains, the thought of even choking down cereal was too much. Instead, he looked at his husband who was staring at nothing and it was the realization that he had no idea what Mike was thinking that forced him to speak.

"We can't stay here, Mike. It's time to go."

"What?" Mike asked, shaking his head as though Eric hadn't been sitting there for the last twenty minutes.

"We can't stay here," Eric said again, leveraging himself out of his chair to keep from falling asleep.

"That's crazy," Mike said, waving a dismissive hand.

"We almost lost her today, Mike. Do you get that? We almost lost Iris. You really want to see who we lose next?"

"It was an accident. Kids get stuck, that's what they do. The way she likes to explore everything? It was bound to happen. She's fine."

"No, she's not." Eric pushed on. "And neither are we."

"Let's not be hasty." Mike held up both hands. "I'll get some boards and nail that crawlspace shut in the morning. End of story."

"It's not a crawl space, Mike. It runs the length of the whole house. I could stand up in there without even touching the walls."

"Well, you've been wondering why she's been staying in her room for weeks." Mike smirked, trying for funny, but landing somewhere closer to condescending. "Now you know."

"It's more than that!" Eric exclaimed. "I found... I found these *patches* cut into the old wall, Mike. I think they were... They were *eyeholes* somebody used to spy on the rooms."

"Iris never said anything about—"

"If she'd have been a bit taller, she might've. Mike, haven't you ever wondered why we never found curtains for the girls' rooms? Why there were boxes of curtains and drapes for every room in this house except theirs? It makes no sense. Unless... Mike, what kind of person would do this?"

"Oh, c'mon. Don't tell me you're afraid somebody's hiding in the walls. I'll admit, it's weird but—"

"Weird doesn't even begin to cover it, Mike. I don't feel safe here. *None* of us do. Iris basically cried herself to sleep, she kept going on about how the house wouldn't let her out."

"She's a kid, it's just her *imagination!* After all the work we've put into this place, we can't just abandon our investment!"

"Abandon our... Oh, for god's sake, Mike! Will you pull your head out of your ass for a minute? I'm not talking about abandoning it. I'm talking about selling it. Right now, this week. We find a place to stay and sell it for whatever we can get. With the improvements you've made, we're bound to get something back, all that matters is keeping us *safe.*"

"And where do you think we can go? In case you forgot, our apartment is gone."

Eric goggled at Mike. The answer was so simple. "Then we get a place here in town."

"*In town?*" Mike howled, and the look on his face was almost funny. Eric imagined it was how the landed gentry might've exploded after being told they needed to go bunk with the peasants.

"Why not?" Eric asked, half laughing but too pissed off to stop. "I've seen rooms for rent all over town. It wouldn't be ideal, but we could make it work until we figure things out."

"Great, that's just wonderful! And while we're throwing money out the window *again,* everyone in town will know we couldn't hack it."

"Mike, this isn't about what everyone else thinks! It's about our family. All of us ran through the house tonight, yelling our heads off, and we nearly lost Iris right under our nose."

"She had to have heard us. She was just playing possum so she wouldn't get in trouble."

"See? That's just it." Eric jabbed a finger at Mike. "The entire time we were looking for her, Iris said she never heard us, not once."

"So?"

"*So?* God couldn't have missed the ruckus we made!"

Mike gripped both sides of his head and let out a growl. "Look, we're talking in circles here, okay? I've got a pounding headache, and I can barely think straight. Let's just punish her and be done with it."

"I *am* punishing her, Mike. And I've got a headache too. But you're not getting what I'm saying."

"Then what the hell are you saying?"

Eric drew a deep breath, like a swimmer attempting a dive they weren't sure they'd survive. For a heartbeat, he hesitated, afraid that he'd already gone too far. But a quick flick of his fingers was all it took. The pain which rocketed up his arm convinced him otherwise. He looked down at his hand and grimaced. One Band-Aid hadn't been enough. He'd wrapped gauze around two fingers from tip to knuckle and then bound them together with tape but still...the blood leaked through.

Eric let out a breath nice and slow, then looked Mike square in the eye. "I asked Iris how she found the 'crawlspace'. She told me the *house* showed it to her the day we got here."

"Scribble... I don't have time for this," Mike said, letting his chin drop to his chest.

"Make time for it," Eric pressed.

"Why should I?"

"*Because I believe her!*" Eric roared, knocking back his chair as he glared at Mike.

From upstairs, Iris's voice called down, plaintive, frightened, the kind of sound that brought most parents running. For a moment, Eric let what he said lie, hoping that Mike would see what he *wasn't* saying all the more.

The words, *I'll leave without you*, were buried beneath the surface. *Please don't make me.*

In the shadows of the kitchen, Mike's face was conflicted, which disheartened Eric more than if he'd just shaken his head.

Tears threatened but Eric managed to fight them back. Iris needed him, and it wouldn't do to let her see her papa crying, not after everything she'd been through.

As Eric trekked up the stairs, calling to Iris that Papa was on the way, he heard Mike muttering to himself. He couldn't quite make out the words and didn't care to try. Mike wasn't following him and that was all that mattered. The further up he climbed, the more Mike's voice became an organic white noise, as though the house was settling in its sleep.

15
ME

I WOULD HAVE SAVED them all if I'm being honest. But they'd left me with no choice. Some lessons were too important not to teach. I'd learned that from Mother long ago.

A Cruel One had slithered his way in, and it was up to me to deal with him. But maybe it was luck that brought him near. If I'd been any other creature, I might have said providence. But whatever the reason, the Cruel Boy pedaled his way toward me the morning after Iris' 'disappearance'. His face was so creased by faux concern I wanted to peel it off like tree bark and leave it to rot at my foundation.

The moment Emily saw him pull up, she gave him a smile as wide as the fields around me. Poor thing. She had no idea how close to ruin she truly was.

"Hey!" she called to him, too young and foolish to be anything but happy.

"Hey, I got your message," he replied. "What happened? You okay?"

"Yeah, yeah, we're okay. My sister just..." she paused, and her face fell, her shoulders caving under the weight of memory.

"My, um... My sister disappeared last night."

"What! Wait, you mean, like—"

"She's back now," she said, rushing to reassure him. "Sorry, I didn't mean... Sorry, nobody slept last night. We're still just really freaked out."

"What the hell happened?"

Emily ran a hand through her hair. "They said she got caught in a crawlspace, but I heard my parents arguing about it last night. It wasn't a crawlspace, it was... I don't even know. She was gone for forever. God. I didn't think we'd... I didn't think we'd get her back."

To give credit where credit is due, the Cruel Boy knew enough to let the moment stretch before continuing to ape sincerity.

"Is she okay?" he asked, stepping in like a predator on the hunt.

"She's with my papa," Emily replied, her eyes locked on the gravel. "They're in town looking for a place to stay. We're, um... We're leaving."

"Good," the Cruel Boy replied in an instant, causing Emily to gawk at him. This time it was he who rushed in.

"I mean... Hhhh, look, I know you guys just moved here but...this place is *weird*, all right? I mean, I'm gonna, y'know, miss—"

A heavy thud shook me from base to crown.

"What was *that*?" the Cruel Boy barked.

"My dad," Emily answered, her voice full of melancholy..

"What, is he packing?"

At first, Emily didn't answer, just glanced back over her shoulder. There was no way for her to know it, but Michael was dragging a large vanity across my basement. It had belonged to Margaret and would look perfect in Emily's room. There were drawers for powders, creams, even kerchiefs. Everything a young lady needed.

I couldn't understand why there were tears in Emily's eyes as she went on.

"I don't think he's coming," she whispered and even the Cruel Boy had no answer to this. "My dad... My dad walks around this place like he's forgotten we're here. I try to talk to him and he just...doesn't even *see* us anymore."

"I'm sorry. Do you...know where you're going?"

"Not yet," she replied, so drawn and mistakenly miserable.

"Is there anything I can do?"

I shuddered again as Michael dragged the vanity to the base of my stairs. Without needing to be told, he wrapped thick straps around his chest and shoulders, because like me, he wanted everything to be perfect. Emily only wiped away tears with the back of her hand.

"Will you come with me?" she murmured. "Help me get outta here for a while?"

"Sure, where?"

"I don't care. I just... I *need* to get out of here."

He laid a hand on her shoulder. "No problem," he said.

"Thanks. That means a lot to me."

Together they stepped inside, but Emily caught the way her Cruel Boy kept checking every corner.

"God, you really are scared of this place, aren't you?" she asked with a smile.

"Everybody I know is scared of this place."

Emily chuckled. "That's funny coming from somebody who used to break the windows."

The Cruel Boy blew out a breath. "I knew I shouldn't have told you that story."

"But you did," Emily answered, smirking. . "Vandalizer."

"Ugh! I only did it *one time*, and it was just cause my brother was ragging on me!"

"Uh huh, yeah sure," Emily teased.

"I didn't... Hhhh. Okay, when I was little, my brother and his friends used to sneak out here and screw around. One day I went with 'em. I thought it'd be fun, but then they started ganging up on me, trying to get me to do something stupid."

"Like throwing rocks?" Emily asked and she had the nerve to appear happy at this.

The Cruel Boy hedged, running a hand across his face. "It was kinda more than that actually."

"Oooooh, do tell!" Emily cajoled. How I hated the excitement in her voice.

"Hhhh, the dare was, get as close to the house as you could and then break something big, like a grandfather clock or something."

Emily screwed up her face. "The house was totally empty when we got here. All the breakable stuff was down in the basement."

The Cruel Boy nodded. "Which tells you how many people actually *got* close to the house."

The two shared a laugh.

After a pause, Emily gave the Cruel Boy a secret grin. "So...how far did you get?"

The Cruel Boy huffed and, for a moment, looked proud of himself. "The front porch."

Emily's eyes lit up at that. "Must've been scary."

He shrugged. "It was either that or get beat up. Anyway, I was trying to make it to the front door, but there was this big *thump* and I freaked out. I...threw the rock and ran. My brother laughed at me the whole way home."

Emily put her hand on the Cruel Boy's arm. "Hey, at least you made it to the porch. Bet your brother never even made it past the yard."

With a snort, the Cruel Boy shook his head. "Way he tells it, he made it all the way to the parlor and Old Lady Horror kissed his ass."

Emily burst out laughing and for the life of me, I couldn't understand how she could sound so joyous about the pain I endured. I remembered the Cruel Boy's brother. Emily wasn't far off. He hadn't made it past the yard but he'd been big enough to make his friends keep their mouths shut about it. Regardless of how close they came, both of them injured me. They'd broken my eyes and scratched my skin. They'd *gouged* me and I would never forgive them.

More than anything, I wanted this conversation to end, but as Emily reached out and took the Cruel Boy's hand, it occurred to me I had an opportunity that might never come again.

"I'm sorry," the Cruel Boy said, which had to be the most duplicitous words he'd ever spoken in his life.

"For what?" Emily asked.

The Cruel Boy shrugged. "I don't know. I'm just sorry. For everything you guys are..."

Emily blushed. "It's okay. Staying here hasn't been all bad."

Before he could say anything else, Emily brought her face close to his. The kiss lasted only a second or two, but it affected him like lightning. He stood there as though his feet were nailed to my foundation.

As Emily stepped back, she laughed with real warmth at the look on his face. "Let me just grab my jacket," she said.

Then with quick, buoyant steps, she bounded up the stairs, leaving the Cruel Boy alone with me.

At last.

He stayed where he was, close to the door. In her room, Emily giggled as she fixed her hair in the mirror. She was so wrapped up in herself she didn't notice I'd closed the door until she heard the lock click behind her.

Confused, she shrugged into her jacket and walked over, her hand dry and firm on the handle.

"What the hell?" she asked, twisting the knob this way and that, picking at the lock until her nail bent backward.

"Jace?" she called, pounding at the door. "Jason!" Her hands were slick now, they left little streaks along the wood.

From below, the Cruel Boy looked up. "You okay?" he called. The insipid little fool, still rooted to the spot.

"I can't get my stupid door unlocked!" Emily cried, fighting me for all she was worth.

The Cruel Boy did not move, not at first. Instead, he swiveled his head about as though hoping someone else might come to her aid. It was several long seconds before he uprooted. "I'm coming!"

His steps were slow. He was scared and trying to hide it. It was almost sweet in a pathetic way. He climbed the stairs one hesitant step at a time, even as Emily's pounding became more frantic.

"Emily? Emily, I'm—"

At the top of the stairs, I made a sound and he stopped. It wasn't a large sound, but then again, it didn't have to be. . Even Emily froze when she heard it.

"Jace? What was that?" she called, her ear pressed to the wood.

He didn't answer her. Couldn't, I think. His eyes were too fixed on the bathroom door I was closing. He twitched as it shut, the silence that followed like an escaped breath. It made the slamming of Iris's door sound like cannon fire in the distance. He jumped, his face twisting as cheek, eye, jaw, and tongue became distorted in fright.

"Jason? Jason!" Emily shouted, but her would-be savior was rooted again. He shook as I threw every other door open hard enough to crack the walls behind them. Some nearly tore free of their jambs when I closed them again.

The Cruel Boy yelped and backed away, the hero in full retreat. I sent little creaks and groans at him until his back was to the balcony rail and then... Well, what I did next was not without pain.

The nails Michael had driven were deep, the new wood hard and inflexible. Ripping it out...my goodness. It really was like pulling teeth.

I will never forget the look on his face when the rail gave way. Or the wail he let out as he fell. His wide eyes and flailing limbs. Too precious. And when the top of his head struck my floor... Oh, what a sound! Like fine porcelain. I'd have cracked myself in half to hear that again.

In the end, the cost was high. I'd not only destroyed Michael's handiwork but ruined a rug older than the Cruel Boy as well. For a moment, I held out hope it could be salvaged, but there was no saving it. Not with that much blood.

Michael would fix everything soon. But right then, I needed to deal with Emily.

Her voice was so quiet as I unlocked the door. She'd heard the crash, she must've known how terrible it was. A part of me wanted to keep her locked up. Hold her there until the body could be carried away.

But a lesson had to be taught. She needed to *see*. So I allowed her to escape. Let her scramble toward the rail and look down and...poor child. She couldn't have known her screams were necessary. Or that she would forgive me. It's true. They would all forgive me one day. Because that's what it means to be family. We learn and we forgive. No matter how many lessons it takes.

16
ERIC

It was wrong of him and he knew it, but the thought was too *there* to fight against. In a town this small, he'd expected the sheriff to be shit-kicker fat.

But he, like everything else, wasn't what Eric had expected. Instead of a portly, good-natured Slim Pickens, the sheriff turned out to be a short, slim, perfunctory man whose watery blue eyes gave only the impression that he cared, not the sincerity.

"We'll need your daughter to make an official statement. You can just bring her down to my office and one of my deputies will take it from there." With well-practiced ease, he slipped a piece of paper out of his shirt pocket. "This is a list of places you can stay in town. If you need help packing, one of my men can stay behind and give you a hand."

The paper might once have been legible but, over time, had been copied and recopied until the letters were hazy. Much of their importance washed away by a bureaucratic rain. The sheriff said something else then, but it skipped through Eric's head so fast he wasn't sure it ever stopped. It seemed like before he could blink, the sheriff had rounded up his men and wrapped up the scene as though it was only one of a dozen he'd dealt with before. And maybe it was. The man, this *stranger*, had moved through their home with familiarity. Eric wanted to laugh at the way he kept checking every corner.

At the bottom of the paper, were the last off-kilter words which could still be read: WITNESSES ARE REQUIRED TO GIVE STATEMENTS WITHIN TWENTY-FOUR HOURS.

Eric glanced inside. Their 'witness' lay curled up in a ball on the couch and though the paramedics had given her a mild sedative, she was still wide awake. She'd almost started screaming again when Eric tried to take her up to her room.

On the floor in front of the couch, Iris sat cross-legged, sword in her lap. Her hands shook and her breathing was panicked at best, but she hadn't moved from her guard post since Emily put her head down.

After the last official had driven off... and they'd taken poor Jason away, Eric wandered into the foyer to find Mike looking up at the shattered railing. Beneath him, the hall carpet was gone and there was a reddish-brown stain three inches from the toe of his boot.

Mike's eyes were stricken. "We're going to need new posts and a rail," he lamented. "And the runner is ruined, there's no way I can salvage that. I'll have to rip out the whole thing and start—"

Eric punched him dead in the face. Pain exploded in his two bandaged fingers but he didn't care. Mike's head snapped back and for a second, he staggered as Eric socked him again like a cat tearing its way out of a fight.

"*What the hell is wrong with you?*" he screamed, drawing back his arm, ready to beat Mike to the floor if he had to.

"*How can you just—*" he struck again, a long overhand haymaker that Mike caught easily, his callused grip stopping it dead in the air.

In the silence that followed, they just stared at each other. Eric's lungs were scorched , but Mike looked, if anything, puzzled. As though he couldn't, for the life of him, understand the meaning of this.

His nose was crooked, his lips were split, but he didn't cry out. Instead, he turned his dull, loveless eyes to the fat red drops rolling softly off his chin.

They spattered against the varnished floor, each drop making a little *plip* as it landed. Mike stripped off his shirt and knelt, his husband and friend already just another part of the house.

"Get me some bleach and a toothbrush," he said without looking up. "Do you have any idea how hard it is to clean blood from between the slats?"

This last piece he grumbled, his fingers scraping the shirt across the floor even as more blood dripped onto his hands. For his part, Eric didn't move, only stared down at his husband, his fury mutating into a revulsion that made him wonder what Mike's head would look like if he stomped on it right then.

Would it squish? Become this wretched mass of pink, red, and gray smeared across the floor? Or would it shatter like old pottery? If he crushed Mike beneath his foot... Would there be anything left?

Without a word, Eric left this stranger on his knees.

Crossing to the couch, he wasn't even surprised to see Dierdre—Old Lady Horror—back in her place of power above the mantle. Instead, Eric knelt and put a hand on both of his daughter's shoulders, hating how exhausted they looked, but there was no time to stop.

"Stay here. I'll be right back."

"Papa? What—" they both asked at once.

"We're leaving, my loves. I'm going to grab a few things. I need you both to stay here and keep an eye on each other."

The dimple in Iris's chin wobbled but she nodded all the same. She even sat up straighter and gripped her sword with both hands. Eric had never loved her more in his life. After a quick hug and a kiss, Eric looked at Emily who was staring at Mike, still on his knees cleaning the floor. In that moment, those eyes were far too young to look that old. They flicked back to Eric and Eric had to fight not to cringe. The fear he saw. The uncertainty. That look would haunt him and he knew it. But they had to get moving *now* or not at all.

Keeping his gaze steady, Eric shook his head and hoped what he wasn't saying would come across. With a trembling breath, Emily nodded and reached out, wrapping an arm tight around Iris's shoulders. Eric almost burst into tears. The knowledge that he was forcing one to look after the other pushed so much sickness into his stomach, he wanted to throw up, but there was no time, no time, no time. He could have his nightmares later. Much later. Right then... packing had to come first.

Eric took the stairs two at a time. Within minutes, he had a suitcase set aside for Emily, enough for three days at least. Dropping it out in the hall, he did the same for Iris. Once finished, he ran into his own room, careful to keep his thoughts on what he needed and not on what he was leaving behind. The things they'd owned since before the girls were born, the photos of their honeymoon on the dresser.

He moved like a robber, grabbing only what was most valuable, the little they could carry. He told himself everything else could be replaced, that nothing mattered but the two lying downstairs, and halfway through his suitcase, Eric almost believed it, but the click of the door closing behind him brought him up short.

Eric whirled, terrified that Mike would be there blocking the way. But there was no one. Forcing himself to ignore the acidic taste of fear, Eric stuffed his wallet into his pocket, snapped the suitcase shut and strode for the door.

The knob refused to turn. It fought him, the heavy brass resisting the sweat on his fingers. Grunting, Eric dropped everything and twisted with both hands. The knob gave an inch but still it fought him, as though someone on the other side were struggling to keep him confined.

With a growl, Eric twisted until he heard the latch slide out of the jam. Cursing , he wrenched backward but the door only slid free an inch.

Eric hauled with everything he had, his arms burning with effort until a thin shaft of light appeared and he hooked his fingers around the edge.

"Mike!" he cried because it could only be him on the other side. "Mike, for god's sake, let go!"

No answer. Instead, the door jerked forward with amazing strength and Eric shrieked as it closed on his fingers.

"Fuck, you son of a bitch!" he howled, but wouldn't let go.

Bracing his foot against the wall, Eric reared back, his shoulders cramping. From far below, Iris screamed and Eric lost all coherent thought.

"Papa!"

Deep within the house, there came a crash, a great splintering tear but the door and the pain carried Eric's thoughts away. Snarling like an injured cat, he pulled harder, his fingers slick with more than sweat. He almost laughed at the thought of the wood turning red.

"I'm coming, baby! I'm coming!"

He pulled, twisted, screamed, and howled, the pain such that he thought he'd lose his fingers, but then the door gave way and he flew backward, his head cracking into the foot of the bed.

Dazed, gasping for breath, Eric ignored his red strained hands and scrambled out the door.

His shoulder clipped the doorframe, his shoes skidding along the floor, but he got ten steps before he stopped, hands flying to his mouth, the coppery taste of blood on his lips.

The thing on the stairs should not have been, not in any way he knew.

It had no eyes, only teeth and bits of gray flesh clinging to its bones. There were roots twisted into its hair, moss growing green and slick along its skull, looping down to a dress that might've been cream and gold once upon a time. It lumbered its way down the hall, extending hands that had been broken and left unmended too many times, its nails grown long and jagged.

Facing the thing, Eric knew who it was. Who it had to be. And he knew why the family plot had been left to fester in weeds and rocks. Margaret was here. Right in front of him. They all were here. None of them ever really left this place. Not the home they'd loved so much.

Eric turned to run but there was nowhere to go.

A scream from below, Emily's this time, pulled him out of his fear. The sudden guilt he felt at almost abandoning her family drove him toward the thing that had crawled up from this nouveau hell.

Tucking his chin, his shoulders rounded, he slammed into the thing like a train. Its nails clawed at his back as they tumbled to the floor, the smell of rot so thick it could've pulled Eric's tongue out by the root.

Eric hissed as Margaret left a burning scratch along his spine. Margaret's mouth was full of black dirt but still she struggled to speak. Scrambling to his knees, Eric clamped both hands over his ears, knowing that if he listened, if he understood, he'd never leave this house alive.

Rolling off the creature, he snarled as its claws hooked into his thigh. With both hands, he wrenched at it, his stomach rioting as the malformed hand snapped free. Gasping in pain, Eric spun away with someone else's bones clutched in his fists.

At the top of the stairs, a twisted laugh tried to escape him. The rest of the family were coming for him now.

Lucas, with his dusty, opaque monocle and his top hat pock-marked by weeds. He shambled up the stairs gripping a haft of wood at his side. Behind him stood little Millicent, one of Mike's hammers in each of her fists. She smiled up at Eric with fat little worms sliding between her teeth. Choking back a sob, Eric looked behind him. Margaret was already struggling to her feet. Dropping her hand to the carpet, he didn't give himself time to think.

He took two stuttering steps back and then ran at the ruined balcony rail.

He leaped.

His knees bent, breath held, the things on the stairs swiped at him as he flew past.

Pain shot up the back of his neck as he hit the floor. His ankle twisted and his chin clipped the banister.

In the foyer, Mike was right where Eric left him, rag and spray bottle in his hands. He didn't even look up as Eric landed.

Behind him the kitchen door started to close. Through it, Eric saw his daughters clinging to each other, their faces pale and pleading. He cracked Mike in the face with his knee as he ran past, knocking him flat.

The kitchen door swung shut and Eric screamed as he slammed into it, his shoulder bruising to the bone.

He launched himself again but the door didn't give an inch. Behind him, he heard the *clip-thump* of Mike getting to his feet and the creak of dead things making their way down the stairs.

Bellowing a prayer, he hit the door again and again, the sound so loud it rang like church bells in his head. Beyond, his babies cried out and he rammed the door once, twice, three times, while a horrid shuffling inched close behind him.

He drew back one last time, gasped as something sharp gouged his shoulder but by then he was already moving. He barreled toward the door, ready to break *through* it if he had to, but at the last second it flew open, like a schoolyard prank, sending him stumbling into the waiting arms of...

Something punched Eric in the chest, stopping him dead. His nose smacked against bone as roots and fetid hair brushed his cheek. He gasped wetly, his hands clutching a moldy, tattered dress.

Whatever it was, let go of him and Eric limped backward, seeing the thing for the first time. A fleshless figure regarded him, its black dress held up by cobwebs, its jewelry tarnished by dirt and time. Where Deirdre's eyes should have been, dandelions bloomed, gray and delicate, ready for a breeze to carry their seeds away.

Eric tried to howl at Old Lady Horror but the knife in his chest wouldn't allow it.

It was a long and silver thing, with filigree on the handle. The sort of blade reserved only for special occasions, like cutting the cake at a wedding. There wasn't much blood, not yet anyway, only a trickle slinking its way down his shirt. The pain was distant but approaching like a bounty hunter tasked with bringing him home.

In a corner, by the basement door, his babies huddled, their eyes wet with tears. He took a step, testing the pain. *It's okay*, he meant to say but the words burbled into a cough as blood dribbled down his chin.

He tried to take another step but a pair of strong hands gripped him from behind. A solid chest pressed against his back and when Eric looked, he found Mike's once kind eyes staring at him , his lips moving just as Deirdre's jaw worked, revealing twin rows of broken yellow teeth.

"It's all right now," Mike said, his voice sweeter than it had ever been. "Everything is going to be just—"

Don't say it, Eric wanted to tell him, his thoughts shattering against each other. *Run. Please run. Get the girls out of here, get them away. Please just...*

"Everything is going to be perfect," Mike said with rapture , his eyes lost in how beautiful their future would be.

Eric whimpered, his legs trembling but those strong hands held him still. With terrifying ease, Mike lifted him clear of the floor. Deirdre inclined her misshapen head and then Eric was flying across the kitchen. His vision burst into a kaleidoscope of colors as he smashed through the big bay window. He landed in a heap in the backyard, the glass rending him from crown to heel.

It was so warm outside, the grass soft beneath his back. The sun was diamond white in a robin's egg sky, not one single cloud to mar it. Mike came to the window and grinned as Lucas and Deirdre dragged the girls over. Eric's babies screamed through the shattered glass.

The pain receded then even though a part of him struggled to hold onto it. Blinking through blood and bits of skin, Eric tried to sit up but the knife held him as surely as his husband once did.

Even Iris's screams, a heartbreaking thing, drifted away, replaced by the rushing breeze that stirred the strips of his face.

Through one half-cracked eye, he saw Iris fight to climb through the window. Lucas threw her over his shoulder while Margaret and Millicent held onto Emily with three hands. Between blood-tinged blinks, Eric watched Mike throw open the back door and stride toward him, carrying heavy straps.

He trussed Eric up like that old teak side table. His years of moving furniture bearing down like punishments. Eric convulsed as he was hauled onto Mike's back, the heavy straps rendering his skin into long, red rags. With a scream in his chest, Eric tried one last time to sit up but the effort filled his head with a riot of colors and he had to fight to keep the sickness down in his stomach.

Please let me go, he tried to say, while his head rested against the back of Mike's neck. *Please let them go*, he thought, his memories of the girls bursting like sparkles of light in his mind. The gray in Emily's eyes, the white of Iris's smile. He held onto these lights for as long as he could.

But soon enough they faded, ran together, bled into nothing but mud. He knew the moment he was carried into the house because his world dimmed into a bitter, silent darkness. All that was left to him was a strange, persistent scratching.

With the last of his strength, Eric reached up, his fingers brushing roots as bits of dirt clung to his hair. He was being carried down into some kind of root cellar, hidden behind a mountain of furniture.

Tears mixed with the blood then, the pain his only comfort. His last thought was to wonder how long they'd keep him down here. How deep did the house's secrets really go?

But there was no answer. There was only the long, cold, heartbreaking descent as Mike carried him down, down, down.

Into nothing.

17
ME

HE WAS LIKE ONE of his paintings in the end. Dressed in red and glass. Within me, Emily and Iris screamed. I knew they would need time to come around, but I was patient.

In time I'd have Michael explain it to them. Tell them that Eric wasn't really gone. My first family never left me. No one did. And as Michael hung poor, broken Eric among my roots, I knew he would become a part of me. Down among my quiet, his light would shine. Not like it used to, perhaps. But then again, life isn't always what we hope it to be.

We stitch and we bend, we push and twist, always with the best of intentions. Sometimes things break along the way, but it doesn't matter. What's broken can be mended. The sullied washed clean.

And eventually perfection, like love, will come to us all. Just like it would come to me and my happy little family.

In the end.

Acknowledgments

Like many authors of any genre, I am indebted to a large number of people. Without their help and encouragement, I would've stopped pushing for my dreams a long time ago. First up, I have to thank my mom for instilling in me a love of reading and for always believing in me. Love you, Momma. I have to thank my dad for teaching me that getting lost isn't always a bad thing. Thank you to my wife for always looking out for me, and to my daughter just because she's awesome, hands down. Thank you to Pam, my friend who taught me how to save my own life.

Thank you to David Niall Wilson, my HWA mentor. He helped me shape this story (and the house) into something truly scary. Another thank you to Patti Moran, who read this book in its earliest draft and showed me how to forge it into something that made sense. Finally, a big thank you to David-Jack and the wonderful people at Slashic Horror Press giving this story the chance to see the light of day. It's been a fun and wild ride, and I can't thank you enough for adopting my baby.

About the Author

Henry Corrigan is a husband, father, bisexual creative, and emerging author who dreams of writing every kind of story. His debut horror novel, *A Man in Pieces,* won the Silver Medal from Literary Titan and was shortlisted for the Top 25 Indie Books of the Year. His horror poem, 'The Litany', was featured in *SHARDS*, a charity mental health anthology from Ravens Quoth Press.

Always an avid horror fan, the first book Henry ever stole was a copy of Stephen King's Night Shift. His mother eventually stole it back. He is a member of the Horror Writers Association and the admin for the Horror Writers Collaborative on Facebook.

As an obsessive, overly anxious person living with depression, he has dedicated himself to providing readers with the diverse, flawed characters that he desperately needed when he was growing up. But above all, he wants to be known for not staying where he's been put. To always surprise people, especially himself. Because that's what makes it fun. The feeling that even he doesn't know what he's going to do next.